Checklist

Vicky White

Contents

Chapter 1

CHAPTER IThe List

□□□·□ □·□□□

Disney men don't exist in real life.

That can be argued as a good thing because of that dude from Pocahontas or Snow White. But then there's Mulan. Tangled. Princess and the Frog. They had my version of prince charming. Someone who cared for you. Loved you. Respected you.

Respect. The word made me choke on a humourless laugh as I stumbled into the bar. Apparently, respecting your girlfriend by not cheating is a hard task. Cheating on me. Two years in a relationship. Almost ten years of friendship all down the drain and into my roommate's pussy, too.

Flashes of Valerie riding Remi on the couch came back to me. The same couch where we watched movies. Talked until dawn. It was also, unfortunately, directly visible from the window next to his front door. Where I stood, jaw on ground, until someone left their bungalow next door.

Now I'm standing inside my favourite bar. I wanted to get drunk.

Even though I lived in a college city that was always packed with energy and excitement, the bar wasn't busy surprisingly. That could be because it was the last week of January on a Tuesday. Midterms were coming up.

"Double shot. Any shot. Please," I begged the bartender the moment my butt hit the stool. My desperation must have been obvious because he looked away from the drink he was making and slowly nodded.

My eyes followed him pour vodka into a tall shot glass before handing it to me. "Enjoy," he laughed while I threw my head back and drowned the drink. I barely recognized the burning taste.

Breathing in through my teeth, I brought the glass back down. "Another please."

The man watched me warily but did as I asked. I swallowed it while the voices in my head warned me that I would regret this. I had class tomorrow, but it started at three in the afternoon. Plenty of time to recover from the hangover I was expecting.

The hangover I was expecting because Remi cheated on me. Remi. Boy next door, helps an elderly woman walk across the street, Remi.

Our mothers would have a field day with this. They were the reason we met since mom worked at Lillian's fashion magazine. They were close friends. And her son cheated on me.

I think I would be more heartbroken if I wasn't so... surprised.

Remi cheated. Some time during my internal monologue, I'd begun laughing—and not a cute giggle. I was manically laughing to myself. That realization made me laugh even more.

"Oh my God," I rasped, unable to stop the chuckles from bubbling out from me. Vaguely, I felt tears streaming down my face. "This is hilarious."

The bartender stared at me with horror. I could tell he was going to cut me off despite only giving me two double shots. Sorry to announce, sir, but I, Althea Selene Carras, am a lightweight.

People saw it as a bad thing, but I saw it as cost-friendly.

Cost-friendly. Being single would definitely save me money.

I laughed harder before wiping my tears away. Hand on chest, I slowly stopped my heaving enough so I could ask the bartender for another shot. For a moment, I thought he would refuse me. That alone was enough for me to stop laughing.

Flattening my hands on the table, I leaned forward and breathed, "I've had a bad night, sir. Please."

He sighed with resignation. I forced myself to hold back my grin of victory.

"You didn't drive here, right?" He cracked a smile when I laughed at his question. Hardly anyone owns a car here. Everything was walking distance if you lived in the area. And most students did. "Just checking."

When his gaze flickered to the seat next to me, his expression flattened and scurried to make my drink. Before his back turned to me, I saw his eyes flare in surprise and nervousness.

Pursing my lip, I glanced to my side and didn't hide my surprise when I saw who filled the seat while I was distracted. And he was huge.

The newcomer was almost freakishly tall, despite sitting on the stool. The muscles in his biceps were bulging in his black turtleneck. Enough that I was sure my hands wouldn't be able to meet if I reached out and cupped it. He looked like someone who owned tattoos, and when my focus drifted to his hands and saw ink exposed on his wrist, I knew I was right.

Finally, my hazy gaze lifted to his face, and this time, I felt the wind get knocked out from me because this man was gorgeous. Dangerously beautiful. And not in the way I was familiar with.

The men I surrounded myself with were soft and lean, with a kind smile and matching eyes. To say this man was the opposite was putting it gently.

His skin had a golden tan despite us being in the middle of winter, and his hair... I was surprised to like it so much. It was nearly black and appeared to be shoulder length, but I couldn't tell for sure because it was in a bun. But his eyes were what got my cheeks burning red.

They were small and downturned but was big enough for me to catch fragments of green. He had hazel eyes, and his lashes were so dark, so curled. It made me instantly jealous before realizing his eyes looked fresh out from a Disney movie.

The thought made me scowl. No thinking of Disney princes' today, Thea.

My focus fell to his chiselled jaw and even stubble before glancing to his full mouth. The last thing I saw was his jaw clenching before he twisted his stool away from me. My mouth opened to strike conversation when a double shot slid in front of me.

I gave the bartender a big grin before drinking the vodka all in one gulp. "Thank you very much."

His smile was faint before he concentrated on the mountain of a man next to me. "You want anything man?"

Next to me, he said gruffly, "Whisky. Neat."

Once again, I was surprised to feel fluttery from the roughness of his voice. He sounded mature. Like a man. Definitely different than the people at my university. Different than him. The cheating mother fucker...

"Why do men cheat?"

It took a second to realize I was the one to ask that question. I didn't know who I was asking, but the man next to me stiffened, so I swivelled my stool and caught his empty stare.

He watched me silently, so I took the chance to explain, "Disney men don't cheat. Actually, maybe they would, huh? I'm sure after the credits roll, they're off to find another doe-eyed girl who can fall for their charms. Maybe the good ones aren't so good after all."

I snorted at my own analogy. "Cheating is cowardly. Especially when you've been in a two-year relationship. You want out, talk. Right? I'm not insane to think that?" Laughing forcefully, I pushed my long hair away from my face. "I need a guy's opinion on this. So please enlighten me."

Again, the stranger watched me, but something different flickered in his blank gaze. Something close to interest, before it disappeared entirely.

"I wouldn't know," his chest rumbled as he spoke, "I never cheated."

"So, it's not hard to do!" I exclaimed loudly, catching some bystanders attention. "Keeping a penis out of another vagina. Who knew?"

"And I know what he's going to say. I didn't celebrate his birthday with him. That will be his excuse, you know? That I prioritized school instead of him, which is completely not true." I threw my arms up in frustration before moving my eyes everywhere but to the man next to me. "I had a weekly assignment due for my ethics class today. And I couldn't do it any other day because she gives us before midnight to finish it. Class ended at six. I told him I had to finish it. It wouldn't have taken me the whole night. I was going to surprise him."

"Instead, he surprised me." I laughed, but it tasted sour. "With one of my friends. With my roommate, to make things even more complicated."

In the back of my mind, I knew I was dumping all of this information to a stranger, but I was tipsy enough not to care.

"And what's funnier? He is terrible in bed!" I could feel more eyes on me, but I ignored them. "Like I'm talking vanilla flavour. So vanilla that you couldn't even taste the flavour. It tasted like cold air. With no satisfying taste. No satisfying finale."

"Before we had sex, I swear it felt like he'd just read an article on some," I rotated my hips, "new moves. Terrible, horrifying execution though."

Not bothering to read his reaction, I turned to my best friend—the bartender—and grinned. "One more?"

He sighed but gave in. "Last one, girl." I watched with glee as he poured me a shot, but I quickly frowned when I saw it was a single.

I was about to argue, but he must have known that because he hastily moved to the opposite end of the bar to serve three women.

With a dragging sigh, I took my last shot of vodka for today. For some reason, it burned more than it was supposed to. I hissed through my teeth before lowering the glass.

"You know what," I said to no one in particular, but something told me my neighbour was listening, "I'm making a sex list. I owe it to myself after all the long-lost orgasms."

Somewhere, I could hear some hushed laughter, but I was busy fumbling with my phone once I took it out of my jacket pocket. I hadn't even taken it off.

I caught a whiff of a spicy, masculine scent that smelt strongly of cedarwood. Absently, I peered to my side and saw the man watching my phone with curiosity.

"What are you doing?" Not used to the gruffness of his voice, my cheeks flushed, but I quickly blamed it on the alcohol before fixating on my phone again.

Opening the Notes app, I made a new note before frantically typing SEX LIST.

The man let out a short, deep laugh before I rambled, "A sex list. I wasn't kidding. I'm tired of vanilla. It's not even my favourite ice cream flavour. I like caramel cookie. I was always a caramel person, but I was stuck with vanilla for two years."

At my scrunched nose, the man hid another amused laugh. I didn't pay him any attention. I was already on number six on my list. My typing was getting more aggressive while I ignored the red lines underneath most words.

He didn't reply, but I also noticed that less people were talking now. Confused, I let myself lift my head, only to watch in surprise as the stranger glared at the people who were watching me. His expression was frightening, and I wasn't the only one who thought that. Everyone hurriedly avoided his gaze and got back to their drinks, but I saw tension lingering on their shoulders before the man studied me.

"A sex list?" he repeated a beat later.

Nodding, I focused on my phone again. "I want all kinds of sex. You would assume a guy knows more than one position but noo. When I asked for prince charming as a kid, I didn't know that meant prince charming was boring. Vanilla. You get where I'm going with this?"

I was hitting number fourteen on my list, but I cringed when I finished typing it down. "Actually, maybe not..."

I pushed my shoulders back, but apparently, I'd gone to hard because next thing I knew, my stool was tipping backward.

My neighbour cussed loudly and wrapped an arm around me. Despite wearing a jacket, I felt how large his hand was against my spine before he ripped himself away from me.

"Jesus, you're a fucking lightweight," he grumbled, sounding almost frustrated with me.

Blinking away my blurry vision, I watched him drown his entire cup of whisky with a small gasp before he slammed the glass down. "Bill. Hers too."

He didn't wait for the bartenders nod before glancing back to me. His eyes seared into mine with intensity. Goosebumps trickled underneath my jaw, instead of feeling intimidated—which is how I would normally feel from this much attention—I smiled.

"You don't have to but thank you." He said nothing as his eyes scanned me with a mixture of confusion and mistrust. "My ex liked to think he was leading the charge of the feminism movement. Said he wouldn't pay for my bill because he wanted to defend my feminism. Sometimes he sounded like he was mocking me. He knew how I felt about supporting girls and all that. But he also knew how much I liked having a choice. And sometimes, I wanted to be spoiled, but I couldn't say that without seeming like a gold digger. He's from a wealthy family, but I also know his family. I doubt that would have made me seem like a gold digger. My parents are well off, too. But..."

I slowly shook my head to get rid of the woozy feeling. It only made it worse.

Cautiously, my hand rose to my forehead before I closed my eyes. "I'm not feeling so great. I'm hitting the decline already. Damn, I'm getting old."

I tried getting out of my seat, but I nearly fell on my face before the stranger scooped me up in his arms again. He was swearing louder now.

"You got someone to pick you up?" He asked, but it sounded more like a demand.

Eyes half open now, I grumbled, "No. Valerie is the one with the car, but we're not exactly on speaking terms right now."

Technically, I could ask Nellie to meet me at the bar since it was a ten-minute walk from our rented bungalow. But I couldn't, not without having to explain to her why I was drinking on a Tuesday night. And I didn't want to talk. Not right now. I wanted to sleep.

The man squeezed my hips and grumbled something under his breath before releasing me.

"Fucking hell." He fished his phone out from his jean pocket and pressed some buttons before lifting his angry hazel eyes to mine. "What's your address?"

I was ready to go on a tangent about stranger danger until I realized he was ordering me a car. I babbled my address and he furiously typed it while clenching his jaw.

"Let's go," he said sternly before putting his hand on a respectful place on my upper back. "The car will be here in three minutes. We'll wait outside."

For some reason, my body blindly trusted this man. The moment he finished carrying me outside, he leaned me against the wall and watched me impassively.

I only smiled. "Will you come home with me?"

He stared at me silently. Soberly. It felt like minutes were ticking away until he threw his head back and scoffed out a sincere laugh.

"Has anyone ever spoken to you about stranger danger?"

"Well, yeah." I frowned and glanced to my boots, slowly coming back to reality before groaning loudly. "You're right. I'm all over the place. Ignore me."

Without thinking, I patted his stubbled cheek once. I lowered my hand, ignoring how it tingled in the process. "You're not a bad stranger, though."

His brow raised, as if he was surprised by that statement. "You're definitely drunk if you think that."

"You haven't tried to grab my ass this entire night. You get an A+ in my book for that," I teased, but that only made his expression cloud in anger.

"Guys grab your ass when you're drunk?"

"Don't worry, I accidentally trip sometimes. And I have a weak knee, so sometimes I just," I thrust my knee out between us, barely missing his crotch, "Move like this."

A ghost of a smile appeared on his lips before it quickly disappeared. "Glad I didn't touch your ass then."

"Glad you have something to be glad about." This felt nice. I haven't thought about Remi in a while.

Until now. Crap.

My eyes started stinging with tears all over again, so I focused on my fury. "I hope it was worth it. The moment his mom finds out about his extracurricular activities, she'll give him hell."

"You know his mom?" He paused, as if he was trying to control his curiosity. "You're going to tell her?"

"No," I snorted before smirking faintly. "I'm telling my mom, and she will tell her friend."

The stranger didn't say anything, but when I turned my head toward him, I noticed him studying me with dim interest again. That was, until the phone vibrated in his pants pocket the same moment a dark grey car pulled to a stop next to us.

In front of me, the man lost all emotion from his face before facing the car. The driver had the passenger window rolled down, and I yawned while he bent down to have a short conversation with the driver. After a moment, he straightened and opened the backseat door.

"Get in," he deadpanned, but his voice softened a fraction when he saw me hesitate. "He will take you straight home."

My shoulder slumped before I pushed myself off the wall. I stumbled toward him and he straightened, as if he was preparing himself to catch me if I fell. I successfully reached him a second later and didn't think twice before throwing my arms around him.

He turned rigid, and I nearly fell when he jerked out of my arms. That made him curse next to my ear before wrapping a big arm around me, holding me steady.

"Such a goddamn lightweight," I faintly heard him growl in irritation, but he still handled me gently as he ushered me inside the car.

Once I was seated, he lifted my legs inside and stepped back to watch me lean against the headrest. I gave him a tired smile. "You're one of the good ones who pretend to be bad, aren't you?" I asked carelessly. "I like you, stranger dude."

He tsked, and for the first time tonight, he smirked, but it wasn't nice. It was mean and malicious. "That's where you're wrong. I'm not nice at all."

At my frown, he strode back and closed my door, sealing his words. I didn't bother to open the door and argue with the man. Instead, the moment the car moved forward, my eyes fell closed and everything went black.

□□□·□ □·□□□

HAPPY RELEASE DAY!!

Chapter 2

CHAPTER IIHungover

□□□·□ □·□□□

I woke up slapping myself in the face. Even though I expected to be hungover, my pounding head had me swearing to the God's that I wouldn't drink anymore so they could take the pain away. Unsurprisingly, my prayers weren't answered.

Begrudgingly, my eyelids peeled open and cringed when I saw sunlight coming into my room. I had periwinkle mesh curtains and for the last year, I've wanted to buy blackout curtains. My window faced the right side of the bungalow, and even though there was a house next to ours, that didn't stop the sun from waking me up at nine in the morning every day.

Nellie and Valerie never had to suffer. Their rooms were on the left side of the house.

The thought of Valerie made me tense. Next thing I knew, I reached for my phone on the nightstand. Unplugged and in front of me, I tapped on the screen. Tears burned my eyes when I saw the messages waiting for me. From Remi.

Hey baby did you finish your assignment?

He sent the text before eight, leaving an acidic taste in my mouth. Did he send this before fucking Valerie? I caught them together at nine.

I continued scrolling through his unread texts, seeing timestamps hours later.

Thea? Are you sleepibg? I thought you couls't come over bexause you had to work. It's my birtdsy. I wnted to see you.

Bavy I love yoi. Im sorrt Im suck.

There was another message. This one came only ten minutes ago.

I missed you last night. Can we meet up today?

Bitterly, I thought, "You didn't seem to miss me while you were fucking my roommate."

But I didn't say that. Instead, I scrambled to his contact and forced myself to ignore his profile picture. It was us as kids. His contact name had a purple heart next to it.

My thumb hovered over the block button. I pressed it hard, sealing our fates.

Eventually, I would have to talk to him. It was the mature thing to do. But I didn't feel mature right now. I wanted to burn his house down, so this was the most reasonable reaction I could come up with.

There was a knock on my door, followed by Nellie's soft, "It's me."

I relaxed against my pillow the same moment my best friend and roommate cracked my door open. Her familiar face made me smile wobbly.

"Fuck," she whispered before rushing toward me. I noted the bottle of pills she was holding, along with an omelette and a bottle of water. She settled everything on my cream comforter before moving my hair away from my face. "You don't look good, hun."

"I don't feel the best," I admitted, taking the pills she handed me before sitting upright. I flinched when the movement made spikes attack my head. "I drank a lot."

There was humour in her voice. "I could tell. You were passed out in the Uber. He had to knock on the door to get me to help you out. By the way, you drooled on his backseat. Never heard an old guy cuss so much."

I cupped my face and groaned. "I'm despicable."

"You didn't throw up on the floor this time, though. Take the win." She offered an encouraging smile before placing the omelette on my lap. "Eat up and take the drugs. Because I need to know what happened to make you spiral on Remi's birthday."

When I cringed again, it had nothing to do with my headache. But I didn't say that, so I did as I was ordered and ate the omelette. My roommate might be majoring in business, but she sure as hell could cook. I've told her more than once to go to culinary school.

Nellie Chikovani was Romanian and Russian, and she managed to get the most beautiful features from her roots. With straight blonde hair that ended above her breast, it contrasted with her naturally golden honey skin. She was tall—taller than me—with almost hooded, nearly black eyes. Her nose, on the other hand, had me jealous at most times. When she turned eighteen, she didn't hesitate to book a surgery to change the structure of her nose. Now, she had a cute little button nose.

We met the first year of high school in our homeroom. It isn't a crazy first-meet story. Remi went to a private school, so I ended up going to my school alone. Nellie had moved from Romania that summer and didn't have anyone to talk to. Thus, making us an inseparable duo, much to Remi's dismay. He never liked Nellie, even though she'd done nothing to him. Heck, she was better than me, with high morals and an even higher judgment for others. Luckily, I was safe from her scrutiny.

After a few minutes, I cleaned off my plate and emptied two pills from its container. Nellie handed me the water bottle once I put them in my mouth.

"What happened?" She immediately asked once I swallowed.

I cracked a smile. "Impatient, are we?"

"I woke up from my sleep to haul you inside the house. And you couldn't even mumble words, so I've been waiting for this conversation for hours." She paused a moment. "What did Remi do?"

Her demanding tone made me cough a surprised laugh. "What makes you think it was him?"

"Okay, Valerie? Did she film you without asking again?" Our roommate was a social media star in the making. Her niches included filming a day in my life, and more often than not, I'd be somewhere in the background.

"How about both?"

At my words, Nellie's eyes bulged. Her attention moved over my face, as if to find signs that I was joking. She licked her lips and cleared her throat before standing up.

"Alright, get up. We're getting coffee before I go to class. We'll talk then."

She didn't let me argue. She was already running out my door, her blonde hair flying in the wind before she was gone from my sight.

I squeezed my eyes shut before rolling out of bed. The door to my bathroom was on the wall to my right, also next to the exit. My steps were weak and sloppy before I stopped in front of the mirror, only to choke in horror at my reflection.

Clearly, I hadn't taken off my makeup last night based on my obvious incompetence. The consequences for this were evident because my eye makeup had me looking like a rabid raccoon. I looked how I felt.

For the next thirty minutes, I showered, scrubbed my body raw and washed the makeup off my face. I didn't bother to touch my hair so I shoved it into a bun before stepping into my bedroom naked. I'd lost all motivation to dress nicely, so I ended up slipping on black sweatpants and a navy turtleneck sweater before shoving my feet into warm socks. The headache was still there, but now all I could focus on was my body, and how desperate I wanted to slump to the floor.

But I made it to the front door, where Nellie was already waiting. So once I got into my boots and jacket, we walked ten minutes to the busy street filled mostly of students.

When we got to Drips Coffee, I ordered my caramel latte and paid for Nellie's drink as well before thanking the barista with a smile. I plopped onto the available couch minutes later, coffee in hand.

Glancing over my shoulder, I stared out the window and lingered my gaze on the lively street before taking a hesitant sip of the drink. Next to me, I felt the couch sink from someone's weight.

"Alright, spill," she ordered before gulping her iced latte. Iced. In the middle of winter. "What did he do?"

Reluctantly, I turned my head and met her impatient gaze. "How long do you have?"

□□□·□ □·□□□

For the next twenty-something minutes, I explained the entirety of last night. Starting from me submitting the assignment to getting all dressed up for Remi's birthday surprise. She hadn't been surprised when I said he cheated—she also didn't like him—but when I mentioned he'd done it with Valerie, she gaped and jumped out from her seat.

"I'm going to kill her," she seethed while I tugged her back down.

"That fucking bitch," she continued, ignoring my flinch before drinking half of her coffee. "I can't believe she did that to you. Especially because you're the reason she lives with us."

I stifled a smile while she rolled her eyes. Nellie didn't like most people, but she warmed up to Valerie when I introduced them first year of university. Valerie was in my program—Journalism—and also happened to live on the same floor as me. It was a friendship waiting to happen.

But then I caught her fucking Remi.

How long was it going for? Was that the first time, or were they doing it behind my back from the beginning?

"What are you going to do?" Nellie's question made me focus on her. She narrowed her eyes on her knees. "We can kick her out of the lease. I can call our landlord today."

"Nels—"

"Allie," she barked, using her nickname for me. "You can't let her live with us after she slept with your boyfriend."

"I'm not saying that. But I'm still a little bit drunk from last night." I winced and rubbed my forehead. "I can't think about this right now. I'm still... surprised, I guess. He's a good guy. He's supposed to be a good guy."

Her face scrunched in confusion. "I'm not surprised, though. He tried so hard to act good. It was only a matter of time before he showed his true colours."

"You think he acted good? You're saying good people don't exist?" I teased, sitting back.

She raised her shoulder lazily. "They exist, but they're complex. Good and bad. It's not black or white. Remi tried so hard to be like those cartoons you watch. As if he thought if he acted like prince charming, you'd date him."

That made me pause. "You think he pretended for two years?"

"Yeah." She snorted, tucking some hair behind her ear. "Ever since I've known you, Remi has been obsessed with you, and you never gave him any thought until second year."

"But it had nothing to do with him being good."

"He literally bathed you in gifts. I've never heard a guy use all the synonyms for beautiful in a day before."

"But I wasn't with him because of that," I frowned. She made it seem like I was shallow. "You know why I agreed to date him."

She sighed and nodded but said nothing else. I knew how Remi felt for years. Most girls know when their guy best friend has feelings for them, but we just ignored it and hoped they move on. Remi never moved on. But at the start of second year, he asked me out. Maybe I was tired of arguing because I agreed. But I think it's because of this sense of doom I always felt—that we'd eventually fall in love because we were the classic love story you'd read in books.

Our moms were friends. We grew up together for almost a decade. A classic best friend to lovers. My own happily ever after. I just had to let it happen.

Only it ended differently. Disney men didn't cheat, but this wasn't Disney.

God, those movies really messed up my expectations. Flynn Rider messed up my expectations.

"Maybe something is wrong with him," she offered before jokingly pointing to her head. "You know, up here. Maybe his bio is all wrong."

"His biology?" I laughed at her explanation. "Well, he's adopted, so we'll never know if his parents gave him something."

"Gave him something? You make it sound like they gave him cooties."

I flipped her off before drinking more of my coffee. She checked the time on her phone and groaned. "Anddd, I have to go. I'm meeting with my professor before class."

"The hot one?" I said louder than intended.

She shushed me, her face turning beet red. "You talk too loud sometimes, Allie."

"And you talk too mean sometimes, Nellie." I smiled at her glare before ushering her to leave. "Go. Ogle him for me. Sneak a picture. Whatever."

She opened her mouth to argue—probably to say that was inappropriate—so I mustered my best puppy eyes before pouting my lip. "Please. I'm all heartbroken. I can't scorn all men."

When she let out a rough breath, I knew I had her. But she still hesitated when she reached the exit.

Smiling, I blew her a kiss. "Go. I'll be okay. I'll need a whole hour to erase the man off my phone."

Cautiously, she pushed the clear door open but didn't move her gaze off me. "Text me whenever. I'll be home before you, so I'll make us something to eat."

"We can watch a movie!" At my grin, her eyes narrowed at me pointedly.

"We're not watching Disney." Before I could open my mouth to argue, she sprinted outside and strode in the opposite direction of me. I watched her through the window before letting out a sigh. Finally, I could lose my smile.

The ache in my chest became so noticeable that I couldn't help but rub a palm over my heart. With a sharp intake of air, I forced myself to take another long sip of my coffee in hopes to distract myself. I tried not to think of Remi—who I thought I could trust. Even though I'd forced myself to accept our relationship, he had been my friend. I thought he was a good guy.

For a moment, I cringed at the idea of telling mom we broke up. Imagining the explosion that would follow, I silently cursed at Remi.

I was too busy contemplating how to break the news to her that I didn't notice someone new strolling into the coffee shop until they stopped in front of the register. Despite wearing a jacket, goosebumps rose on my arms when I heard a vaguely familiar voice order gruffly, "Medium latte."

Two words, but it was enough for me to flatten myself against the couch, praying that I would be absorbed and hidden away from the man's sight. Another prayer that wasn't answered because the moment he started to walk toward the opposite end of the bar, his disinterested expression swung toward me.

His steps faltered, but that was the only thing that could offer what he was thinking. The stranger from last night watched me before lowering his eyes to the coffee in my hands. His eyebrow rose for a millisecond before his face returned to normal.

A surprised gasp got lodged in my throat when he took three long strides before stopping in front of me. I nervously cleared my throat while shakily bringing my coffee back to my lips, hoping if I ignored him long enough, he'd walk away.

Another prayer unanswered.

"I'm surprised you're standing." His tone implied nothing, and when I reluctantly lifted my head, I met his bored gaze.

Realizing he wasn't trying to tease me from last night's events, lines sketched my forehead. He sounded almost rude, even though his accusation held no emotion.

Before I could ask him what he meant, the barista behind the bar called out, "For Myles," before laying the coffee on the table.

My lips parted but before I could make a sound, the man in front of me twisted and marched to the bar. With sharp precision, he swept the coffee off the surface before stalking to the exit, not sparing me another glance.

I hadn't realized I'd gotten up until I was pushing the door open. "Hey! Wait!" I called out to the man—Myles, I figured—who crossed the street with long strides.

He stopped when he reached the sidewalk. By the time I stood in front of him, I was breathing out raggedly. "Hi," I managed to stammer before gripping my hip. "You don't have great social skills, huh? Do you always approach women, say one sentence to them, then leave without waiting for a reply?"

Myles cocked his head before stepping around me. My jaw fell to the floor when he continued walking in the direction of my school. In the back of my mind, I briefly wondered if he was a student before catching up to him again.

"Okay, not a talker, huh?" I chuckled breathlessly before hopping in front of him, so he couldn't escape me. "Before you make any judgments of me, just know that," my face scrunched up in embarrassment, "I don't normally make it a habit to get drunk by myself. I'm usually more responsible than that."

He didn't say anything right away, so I continued ranting while adamantly avoiding eye contact. "I also should say thank you. I don't know if I said that last night, but you didn't need to take care of me. Some guys wouldn't be that... respectful when they see a stupid girl by herself, drinking. And I can totally send the money you spent on me. The bill and the driver costs."

I found myself unsurprised when Myles didn't reply, so hesitantly, I tipped my chin up. My cheeks tinted red when I saw that he'd been watching me intently, and I breathed in softly when I took in his appearance. Unlike yesterday, I was sober and no longer in the bar, which had terrible lighting. Even though the sun wasn't out, that didn't stop me from noticing things that weren't obvious the night before.

Like our last encounter, his almost black hair was pulled into a bun but this time I noticed the texture. It looked soft, silky and wavy and my fingers twitched at the thought of touching it before I quickly shot that idea away. His face, however, seemed more intense up close. All the ridges were sharp along with his jawline. His cheekbones were high, and his tan skin was somehow darker now. Despite the shade, I faintly noticed some freckles trickling around his cheeks. And he was tall—which was evident enough by how far I had to crane my neck.

Yes, I was five-foot-six. Average height for a woman, I'd say. But Myles was almost a mountain, nearly a foot taller than me. I'd probably put him at around six-foot-four, making him officially the tallest man I've met. Not only that, but he was the biggest, and definitely the most intimidating man I've ever met. Not because of the bulging muscles that was way too noticeable underneath his jacket, or the tattoos that crept onto his hands and neck. But by his expression—or the lack thereof.

Finally bringing my gaze to his, I paused in admiration. Hazel eyes were always so pretty, and in this lighting the green was brighter. Until his eyes darkened and narrowed, bringing me back to reality.

"Can I go?" He asked coolly, although it sounded more like a statement.

Rapidly, I blinked in realization that I'd been blocking a door with my body. And his hand was gripping the handle.

Instead of moving away like I should have done, I glanced over my shoulder and read the name on the door. Blackstone Ink.

"You're getting another tattoo?" I questioned without thinking.

He let out a frustrated breath, and for some reason, the sound made me smile before I turned back to him. I was quickly starting to get accustomed to Myles' personality. He clearly was a man of very few words. He eyed me blankly.

"Work?"

"You can say that."

"So you do? Work here, I mean." I grinned before tilting my head to the side, studying him curiously. "Do you do your own tattoos? Wait, how old are you?"

He tried hard to keep his expression neutral, I'd give him that. But I didn't miss the faint lock of his jaw before he bit out, "If I tell you how old I am, will you let me leave?"

Smiling a crooked smile, I joked, "Well, it depends. Do you want me to leave?"

Instead of answering my question, he exhaled roughly. "I'm twenty-five. Happy?"

Twenty-five? The man looked like he was in his late twenties, at least. Not because he had wrinkles or aging skin, but from his eyes. Staring into them made me feel like I was talking to someone who experienced things no one should experience.

There was that, and the fact he was massive and covered in tattoos. It seems like his face is the only part of his body left unscathed. Definitely not the type of guy I usually associate with, and in normal circumstances, I would have avoided him like the plague. Maybe it's because of pre-existing judgments, but Myles, despite his exterior grouchiness, didn't take advantage of me during my most vulnerable moment. That had to count for something.

"I'm twenty-one," I offered with a smile, even though he didn't ask. "Are you also a student at AU?" AU being Ameria University, which resided in the heart of Michigan, Ameria.

Myles almost smirked before relaxing his expression. "Does it look like I'm a student?"

"Well, there's a ton of students who work on this strip." Plus, we're in a college city. "But I'm guessing that's a no?"

His eyes were too busy scrutinizing me to answer, so I sighed and moved away from the door. "Alright, go ahead. I'll stop annoying you with my questions."

I didn't wait for his goodbye. I turned my back to him and looked both ways on the street before taking a step off the curb. The moment I began to push myself forward, he spoke.

"How's your list?"

I almost slapped myself in the face, both in surprise and humiliation that he remembered.

It took all my strength to slip back onto the sidewalk, avidly avoiding the fast-paced students who were walking to school before stopping in front of Myles again. This time, there was the faintest gleam of amusement when he saw how pale my cheeks have gotten.

"Again, in my defence, you didn't catch me at my finest moment." I gripped my coffee tighter. "I figured out my boyfriend was cheating on me yesterday, and with some... reflection, I impulsively made the list."

He didn't seem to care for my excuses. Instead, he bowed his head closer to mine before asking in a low drawl, "Are you going to go through with it?"

In that moment, I could have lied. Pretend that I had a moment of weakness and deleted it off my phone. But none of that came out. The truth did. "I want to."

If he was surprised by my confession, he didn't show it. His eyes hazel eyes watched me silently while every nervous emotion was evident on my face.

"I didn't experience a lot," I blurted without thinking. "In my relationship, I mean. Not that I wasn't happy, per-say, but the sex was really bland and most of the time, I never had the big explosion. God, I probably shouldn't reference a climax as an explosion, but it's accurate. At least, I think it is? I don't know, I haven't felt one in a long time. At least, by another dude. Before I dated my ex, I'd only been with two other guys who were also severely lacking. I think I'm the problem at this point and... please tell me to shut up."

I wanted to slap my face repeatedly because—I can't believe I said all that. To a total stranger. Again. If he didn't say anything in the next second, I'd probably bury myself in the ground from embarrassment. Nellie often said my filter was broken, but I never thought to fix it because I hardly talked to new people.

Not only was Myles new, but he was different. Really freaking different compared to the people I usually spoke to.

When he didn't respond right away, it took every bit of courage to lift my gaze to his, only to widen my eyes in surprise when I recognized the curiosity on his expression.

"What?" I mumbled.

His lip twitched before it went back down. "I want to help you." When I furrowed my brows, he added, "With your list."

I choked on my spit before stuttering, "W-what?" I coughed when my throat started tightening. I brought the coffee to my lips and chugged. It was getting cold.

Myles shrugged a shoulder calmly. The exact opposite compared to my frantic personality. "I'll be your wing man."

Gaping like a fish, I managed to challenge, "And why would you do that?" Although, I was relieved he didn't want to help me another way.

"New Year's resolution," he deadpanned, but that only made my confusion grow.

"Your New Year's resolution is to help a girl with a sex list after being cheated on?" I said a little louder than necessary.

I ignored some stray glances we were getting from bystanders.

"More like being nice."

"Tomorrow is February." When he stared at me blankly, my nose crinkled. "You haven't done something nice all month?"

Seemingly annoyed by accusation, he glared. "When's the last time you did something nice, princess?"

"Almost an hour ago. I bought my friend coffee." I paused before frowning. "Princess?"

He stiffened, as if he realized what he said. "Well, you were talking about Disney dudes like they existed. Seems fitting." Then, his eyes landed on mine and lingered for a long moment before he rumbled, "Plus your eyes are big."

My eyes widened before I noticed what I was doing. Hastily, I dropped my head and raised a hand to my eyes while insecurity bloomed in my chest. "What's that supposed to mean?"

Myles grumbled a curse, almost as if he was irritated with the situation he was placed in. Maybe don't call a girl's eyes big. That didn't really sound like a compliment, but on the other hand, Myles didn't look like he gave compliments often.

Still avoiding his gaze, I kept my head low but heard him take in a deep breath, as he was readying himself to speak. But he was cut off suddenly when a voice bellowed from the distance, "Althea!"

Next thing I knew, I jerked closer to Myles without thinking twice. Instead of shoving me away like I expected, he gripped my upper arm and steadied me while glaring over my head.

Following his gaze, I hid my flinch when I saw Remi stomping toward us with a furious expression.

□□□·□ □·□□□

Now that two chapters are posted, I can finally give fun facts! Posting will happen Friday's at 5pm (I got a little excited today, aka why I'm posting before 5).

I loved writing this book, and I cannot wait to share Althea and Myles' story. You know I'm a sucker for a grumpy sunshine :')

I hope you loves enjoyed the first two chapters, and I hope to see you next week! Have a great weekend x

Chapter 3

CHAPTER IIIBatman

□□□·□ □·□□□

"What the hell, Thea?" Remi hissed while stomping across the street, looking pissed. Considering the last time I saw him he was cheating on me, I flinched before lowering my head—only to realize Myles was still holding onto me. He noticed the same time as me.

He ripped his hands off my arms, but it was too late. Remi already noticed him.

"Who is this?" He demanded and moved forward, so he was at arms reach. When I didn't lift my head, Remi let out a frustrated sigh before softening his tone. "Listen, look at it in my perspective. You didn't answer my texts. My calls aren't going through, and now I see you're with..." His nose flared with disgust as he looked Myles over, but he quickly fixed his expression before clenching out, "Another man I don't know."

Peering over my shoulder, I saw Myles focused coolly on Remi, but there was a warning glint in his eyes. Taking a deep breath, I faced Remi and stepped away from Myles, keeping him behind me.

For a moment, my eyes lingered over my ex-boyfriend. His dark brown, wavy hair was usually well-kept. With faded sides, it was hard to make it dishevelled without looking good in the process. But right now, it was a mess. And not a pretty, sexy mess. He seemed frantic. Nervous. Scared.

His eyes were downturned, and during most of the day, they were a shining chestnut brown. But staring into them now made it felt like I was swimming in milk chocolate—and I hated it.

Physically and personality wise, Remi and Myles were exact opposites. Remi was my type. He was tall, around six-foot, and lean. He had some muscles in his arms and legs because he played basketball in high school, and he had a faint tan. His nose was straight, and while his facial features weren't baby-like, they weren't as harsh in comparison to Myles. He was clean shaven, which I always liked because when Remi smiled, it felt like it was straight from a Disney movie.

Right now, he felt like the villain.

"Althea," he bit out, losing his patience. He started to step forward the same moment Myles gripped my upper arm again, and we all froze. Remi's eyes narrowed at his hand before his face turned red. "What the fuck do you think you're doing, man? Let go of my girlfriend."

Myles didn't budge, which riled up Remi more. "Let go of her before I make you."

"Remi," I gaped in surprise because he wasn't violent at all.

"Who is he, Thea?" He demanded, not moving his glare off the man behind me. "Are you cheating on me?"

I couldn't stop myself from coughing in disbelief before shrugging Myles hand off me. He released me but didn't stop hovering while I tried to take a slow, deep breath to stop myself from blowing up, even though all I wanted to say was "You cheated on me twenty-four hours ago, maybe even longer than that, and you think you have the right to ask me if I'm cheating?"

Instead, I put on a tight smile before asking a little too loudly, "How's Val's pussy?"

In a matter of seconds. all the fury vanished off Remi's expression as he stared at me with horror. But I kept my smile intact, especially while I stepped closer to him, so he could feel the hatred rolling off my body in waves.

"Well? Tell me. Was she good? Was it worth it? How long has it been going on? Weeks? Months? Come on, Rem. We both know you know how to speak. Tell me about all the ways you cheated on me. Is she the first one?"

"Thea," he rasped but I shook my head.

"Answer the question, Remi."

His eyes squeezed shut before he let out a ragged breath. "It... it was only yesterday. I swear to you, Thea. I swear. It's just, it was my birthday and you weren't there and I was upset. Then Valerie showed up with a bottle, and we ended up drinking the whole fucking thing. I don't even remember it. Fuck. The only reason I know what I did was because we woke up—"

I lifted my hands and pushed him before rushing out angrily, "I don't want to hear it."

"Thea." His eyes were pleading before he reached out for me. I jumped back before he could, and his expression shattered with anguish. "Please. I was drunk."

"So was I, Remi. So was I." I pointed at my chest hard. "I got drunk yesterday after I found you sleeping with my roommate. My friend. Borderline blackout drunk, and you know what I didn't do? I didn't fuck anyone! It was that easy to keep it in my pants." I threw my arms out in frustration. "You cheated. You cheated on me. There's no excuse."

"You didn't show up for my birthday—"

"I was going to surprise you!" I clenched my jaw to stop myself from shouting. More and more people were starting to look our way. "Are you going to say I'm the reason you slept with Valerie?"

He rubbed a hand over his mouth. "No. No. I just felt like I wasn't your priority in that moment. I had a goddamn moment of weakness. Are you seriously going to break up with me?"

"Yes, I am."

This time, he laughed humorlessly before shaking his head in disbelief. "You know what, Thea? You need to fix your expectations. You always want a fairy-tale, but you don't know how the real world works. We have real problems, so we need to fix them. So we should have communicated better, but you're always expecting me to be fucking perfect. I'm human."

"I never said you had to be perfect. But cheating on me isn't a problem that needs to be fixed. There is no fixing something you broke."

"Again with your expectations." He rolled his eyes, and something in me snapped because one second I was throwing my fist toward his face, the next, I was being tugged back.

It took a few heaving gasps of air to clear my blurry vision, and the first thing I saw was Remi's disbelieved expression, but he wasn't holding his cheek or nothing. I hadn't hit him before I got yanked away.

After another moment, I dropped my head and felt my cheeks redden when I saw Myles arm wrapped around my waist in a steel grip. I tapped his arm twice to let me go, but that only made him tighten his hold before I felt him breathing next to my ear.

"Get the fuck out of here before I finish what she was about to start," he threatened tersely before carrying me inside the tattoo shop. I yelped in surprise by how easy he lifted me, but before I could kick him, he lowered me onto my feet and set me down.

Feeling slightly woozy, I hurriedly locked my knees so I wouldn't collapse in the entrance of Myles workplace—which was dimmer than I expected.

"How the heck do you tattoo with this lighting—whoa!"

Myles had my hand in his while tugging me at the opposite end of the parlour. I didn't have a chance to look around before he thrust me into an office. Next thing I knew, he was closing the door behind him and locking it.

I widened my eyes surprise when he turned to me. "What did I do?" I raised my hands playfully in surrender while he glared. He didn't say anything, so I let them drop before checking out the office. "Why are we here? Does this belong to you?"

"So many fucking questions," he grumbled in annoyance but otherwise said nothing else before stomping to the left side of the room, where a bar sat. "You want water, princess?"

"Sure, and stop calling me princess."

He made a noise under his breath, but for some reason, I doubt it was a sound of agreement.

I watched him lower his coffee onto the bar and roughly snatch a paper cup off the table before stopping in front of the water dispenser. For a moment,

I admired how muscular he was, even if his jacket was hiding his back. As if he could feel my gaze, he pushed his shoulders back tensely.

Hurriedly, I shot my head to the L-shaped black desk behind me, which didn't have much of anything besides two monitors. A large, black office chair faced the direction of the windows opposite of the entrance, and through the blinds, I recognized the back of the shop. Behind the chair, covering the whole wall on the right, were three separate industrial storage cabinets.

All the furniture was black. I was surprised that the walls were a dark, dirty green rather than black as well.

"Here."

Myles tatted hand shot in front of my face, making the water splash in the cup from his aggressiveness. Hesitantly, I gripped the bottom while simultaneously avoiding where his hand rested on the cup.

"Thank you." I took a slow sip of the cool liquid before lifting my head to his. He watched me soberly, but I noticed how his eyes tracked my movements assessingly. "What?"

His eyes flared with ire before it went away. "Your boyfriend is a piece of shit."

"And that's why he is my ex-boyfriend." My tone was hostile, but I felt the ache in my chest growing. I lowered my gaze before holding the cup with both hands. "I never expected him to be perfect. I can separate fiction from reality. But still, I thought... I thought he was my own version of prince charming. The realistic version, at least. We were supposed to end up together. That's what our mom's wanted. Heck, that's what movies and books promised. It was my fault for believing they'd promise fidelity, too."

"We've known each other since we were twelve. Twelve. Our moms were good friends, and they made sure me and Remi would be good friends. They never pushed us to be together, but I knew they wanted us to date." Flashes of my past come back to me, but the memories felt like they belonged to someone else. "Remi wanted us to date. Ever since we got to high school. It was easier to avoid his feelings back then because we didn't go to the same school, but university happened and... I caved. I caved because I knew it would happen eventually. And he cheated on me. Remi. The guy who swore to love me forever. It's almost embarrassing, right? That a guy who claimed to love me so much, cheated. There must be something wrong with me."

"Maybe I do have high standards," I whispered but Myles' harsh scoff reminded me that I wasn't, in fact, talking to myself.

"If he can't keep his dick in his pants, that's on him. Not you," he grated through his teeth. "People cheat because they want to break up, but they're fucking cowards."

Cracking a smile, I looked at him over my lashes. "You never cheated, Myles?"

"That would require me to have been in a relationship, princess."

Rolling my eyes at the nickname, I asked, "You've never dated anyone?" I was grateful we were moving the conversation onto him. When he shook his head no, I frowned. "Why?"

"Why? You want to date me or something?" He shot back crudely, almost defensively. "I don't do girlfriends, princess. I keep to myself."

"Well, that sounds lonely. Do you have friends?"

"What's with all the questions?" He grinded his teeth before narrowing his eyes to the storage cabinets. "Need a fucking question jar for you."

"Question jar?" I almost smiled when he turned his glare to me.

"Put a damn dollar inside the jar every time you open that mouth of yours and ask a question."

"It's not my fault you get riled up easily," I joked before shrugging a shoulder. "I'm in journalism. I guess I'm ingrained to ask questions about things I don't know. And you are an enigma."

"That's a big word to a guy who barely finished high school, princess."

Barely finished high school? A question threatened to spill from my lips, but I swallowed it back. I tucked that information for later.

"Mystery. Puzzle. Hard to understand," I explained, sipping some more water. "You don't like talking to me, but you helped me yesterday. You helped with Remi."

He made a low noise. "I never said I don't like talking to you." His gruff sentiment made me jerk my head back in surprise. "And I told you why I helped."

"Ah, yes. Your New Year's resolution." I smiled and cocked my head before drawling sarcastically, "You can give Disney a run for their money if you keep acting so nice."

His face wrinkled in disgust, and I almost choked on a laugh. Apparently, me implying that he was nice did not sit well with the guy. At all.

"Again referencing Disney. They must be shitting fucking gold because I don't get why you like them so much."

"I don't like Disney per-say." Myles gave me a bored expression, clearly assuming otherwise. "I like their movies. I like what they represent."

"And what do they represent? Marrying someone they don't know?"

"No—well, yeah. The earlier movies!" I rushed out when his mouth twitched in a short-lived, satisfied smirk. "Yes, the earlier movies are like that. But still. When I was a kid, it was all I watched." It helped me feel less lonely. "Now, the movies are more meaningful. Come on, didn't a movie ever let you escape from reality?"

His expression flickered with something, but before I could examine it further, he turned his head away. My eyes widened before I grinned. "There is, isn't there?" He didn't respond, still adamant in ignoring me. "Come on, what is it?"

"I won't stop talking until you tell me," I teased, rocking back on my heels. "Heck, I have a list of questions in my head already. I can ask them all day. In alphabetical or—"

"Batman," he gritted, eyes narrowed into slits when he focused on me again. He looked angry—as if he was mad at himself for yielding to my command. "I watched Batman."

My cheeks started to hurt by how hard I was smiling. He glared harder. "What now?"

Shrugging innocently, I said, "You just feel a little more human now. Batman?" I tried to think if I ever watched the movies, but I came out blank. "I don't think I watched it. Is it a series?"

He let out a deep noise of agreement before bringing his hazel eyes to mine. My cheeks rose with colour when he lingered his focus on me. I wasn't used to getting attention from someone who wasn't Remi. Heck, I've never gotten attention from someone like him. Maybe something is wrong with me, but I spent my entire life avoiding people who were like Myles. Someone who towered over me. Someone big and muscular. Tattooed. Intimidating. Someone who was clearly on the wrong side of the tracks.

I didn't come from a wealthy family, but my parents brought in a good income. Living in Detroit most of my childhood, where crimes happened daily, they always encouraged me to stay safe and recognize the potential for danger before I ever stepped into a situation. Myles had the potential.

But right now, with attention only on me, I didn't feel scared because in the two encounters I had with him, he helped me both times.

There was a sudden, hard knock on the office door, and I lurched in my spot.

Blinking back to reality, I glanced at the door and sighed in relief when I saw it still closed. Myles was already moving away from me, ripping the door off its hinges before impatiently barking, "What?"

The person on the opposite side seemed used to his short temper. "Your two-p.m. slot's here."

"And he's fucking early. He can wait."

I kept my grimace at bay. I wasn't shy at swearing, but Myles seemed to do it after every other sentence. "I'll go. I have class in an hour anyways," I admitted, quickly finishing the cup of water before throwing it in the recycling next to the water dispenser. When I turned to Myles again, I smiled when I saw his eyes already on me.

Stopping in front of him, I asked, "What time is it exactly?"

He made a frustrated sound but he still shoved a hand into his jacket pocket and pulled out his phone. The moment the screen lit up and unlocked, I snatched it from his hand.

"What the fuck?" I heard him growl, but he didn't try to take it out of my grip.

Fearful he was going to take the phone too soon, I looked for his contacts list and was immediately stunned when there wasn't anyone saved. Questions were on the tip of my tongue, but I showed restraint. I added a new contact: me.

"What are you doing?" He demanded, but it didn't sound as aggressive as I assumed it would.

Saving my information, I turned off the phone and handed it back to him. "My name is Althea, by the way," I introduced with a chirp. Ignoring his question felt good.

Surprisingly, he didn't make a move to delete me from his contacts. Although, he did glower before grumbling, "Myles."

"Now we're fully introduced," I grinned before skipping to the exit, only to notice the doorway empty. I hadn't even realized the speaker left.

With a short wave, I offered him a smile before stepping out of the office—but not before shouting, "Don't be a stranger!"

I left the tattoo parlour feeling better than I did when I entered.

□□□·□ □·□□□

happy Friday loves! anotha day anotha chapter

I'm getting close to my exams so that means I start to breathe easier soon :') hopefully that also means I can write some chapters

wishing you the best weekend x

Chapter 4

CHAPTER IVSex Club

□□□·□ □·□□□

I know I'm not the smartest bird in the nest, but sometimes I applaud myself for not taking any classes on Friday. Thursday is my new Friday. And because I have no classes on Monday either, I always have an extra long weekend.

Better yet, Thursday is the only class I have with Nellie. Even though her program is in business, she was able to secure news reporting as an elective. Not that I was complaining—I had a friend for the three hour lecture.

"Let's sit in the back today," she begged once we stepped inside the auditorium. It could easily sit two hundred people, and because of the vast size of the room, I didn't like sitting in the back. While the professor did wear a microphone, he also had a thick Australian accent.

Right as I was about to persuade her to sit in the middle instead, my phone vibrated in my hand. I lifted it toward my vision and skimmed the screen while my mouth remained open to speak. But the moment I saw who texted me, I choked on saliva.

With a hoarse cough, I slapped my hand on my chest in hopes that would clear my airway. It didn't.

"Oh my God, are you okay?" She hissed, tugging me away from the doors so I wouldn't be in anyone's way. I sagged against the wall once I managed to stop myself from choking, only to notice Nellie's eyes wide with worry. "What happened? Did Remi message you again?"

"No. No. I blocked his fourth account in the morning." He's going through social media accounts so fast, I'm starting to wonder how many emails are actually his, and which emails he's making up.

A frown marred her lips. "Then what did you see?" She tried to reach for my phone, but I flimsily moved it behind me.

"Mom sent me a naked picture," I lied boldly while Nellie's face paled in horror. Some of my classmates trained their wide gaze toward me, and I fought a grimace before rushing out, "She meant to send it to my dad."

I was dying with embarrassment, but thankfully, she didn't ask for any more details while patting my shoulder comfortingly. "I'm sorry you had to see that, Allie."

Wanting to forget all about this, I pushed myself off the wall while avoiding the attention I've gained. "Yeah, let's... let's sit in the back row." So I don't have to feel people staring at me from behind.

We ended up picking our seats on the far-left corner of the room, thankfully away from prying eyes. I wanted to slap myself in the face repeatedly because—why didn't I just tell Nellie who texted me?

In the corner of my eye, I spotted Nellie taking her laptop out of her bag, distracted with her belongings as she prepared for class. I exhaled shakily before turning on my phone.

Not gonna lie, princess. Wasn't going to text you, but curiosity fucking killed the cat and it'll kill me too. You decided if you're gonna go through that list of yours?

Myles wasn't programmed into my phone—because I didn't have his number—but it was fairly obvious who the message came from. For some reason, I let myself enter an alternate reality where I allowed Nellie to read the message, and I could see everything shattering into pieces. And by everything, I meant my dignity and self-esteem.

Possibly dramatic, but also the truth because my best friend was brutally honest and judgmental. And while I was always safe from her crass words, if she learned who I was talking to—no—if she knew what he was talking about, it would be the end of me. I could hear it now.

"A sex list, Allie? Why would you do that? Don't you have any self respect? Guys already think they can walk all over us as it is, but if you go around sleeping with a bunch of guys, not only is that not safe, but you're going to make a name for yourself."

And she would be right. Even though it was unfair men would be safe from public scrutiny.

Yet, that didn't stop me from texting the tattoo artist.

I've considered it, not gonna lie.

That boyfriend of yours seriously deprived you, huh. His reply was instant.

The image of Remi had me seeing red. Ex-boyfriend, batman. Ex.

You're not planning on making up with him?

Puh-lease. I have more self-respect.

Let me guess. Disney taught you that.

... To be honest, I could totally see Cinderella taking back the dude. I don't even remember his name, but if he cheated, I imagine her letting bygones be bygones.

Which girl is that?

For a moment, I forgot he was clueless about Disney and its princesses. I found it refreshing, although I wasn't sure why.

Blue dress. You should watch her movies!

Movies? There's more than one?

There's three, but we don't acknowledge the second one. The third one however? A-MAZ-ING. The guy actually has a personality in that one.

I'll take your word on it.

You're not going to watch them, are you?

His reply came after a few moments. No. But it's funny that you think I would.

Why? Is your masculinity fragile? The second I hit send, I wanted to slap myself in the face. Repeatedly. Because why would you say that, Althea? Why would you say that?

I was scolding myself when I heard Nellie's chair swivel. "You okay, hun?"

"Yeah," I choked, lowering my phone face-down on the table before clearing my throat. "Thirsty. I'm thirsty."

Her brows rose while I rummaged through my school bag. By the time I pulled my water bottle and laptop out, Nellie snorted in amusement. "You're scarred, huh?"

"What?" I said a little louder than needed before remembering she was talking about the imaginary photo mom sent me. "Oh. Yeah. Totally scarred. I want to dig a hole and bury myself." At least that wasn't a lie.

She patted my shoulder. "Tell your mom just because she has a banging bod, that does not mean she has to send it to her daughter."

My eyes widened in horror. "Are you saying my mom's hot?"

The corner of her mouth rose before she turned to her computer. "If it makes you feel any better, you have her body. And more, actually. You're basically her twin."

I pursed my mouth in disgust before looking at my lap. My hair, which I wore down today, was in my vision. Reluctantly, I had to agree with Nellie—I did resemble my mom.

Honestly, at times, I felt like a bland version of everyone else in the world. My hair was a medium chocolate brown shade, and while it did have some waves, it was boring. I had naturally golden skin—something I also inherited from mom's Greek heritage—and I also had her nose. It was small, yes, but it was also droopy.

Something people always commented on, however, were my brown eyes. They were big and round, so much so that it was the first thing people noticed when they looked at me. I loved them at first, but like every other kid, I had bullies, and they loved to harass me. Push me around.

"Teacher! There's a bug in the class!"

"Where?"

A skinny finger pointed toward me. "There! Kill it!"

The comments stopped when I grew into my eyes, and that only happened when I reached high school. There's a reason I entered high school alone: I had no friends besides Remi, but even he didn't go to my school. Every time I remember the people who taunted me and the people who said nothing to defend me, I get angry because—why would you bully someone over their eyes?

I fought a grimace when I remembered how Myles acknowledged them last week.

To this day, I don't know who I inherited my eyes from. Mom's were almost sultry. Dad's were upturned and small. It is the greatest mystery in my small family.

"If we're twins, we're fraternal," I mumbled before lifting my phone up. I sucked a breath when I saw that Myles actually responded to my message.

My masculinity is well intact, princess. Promise you that. I just don't like fairy tales.

I bit my lower lip as I re-read his text. Myles was masculine and more. I've quite literally never met someone who physically radiated with manliness. Whose voice was as deep as the ocean. Who was built like a machine. I surprised myself by liking it.

Why not?

His reply came the same moment my professor entered the room. Nellie nudged me to turn off my phone and I begrudgingly did, but his words continued ringing in my head.

Fairy tales don't exist. Makes no sense to watch something that gets your hopes up for nothing.

□□□·□ □·□□□

Across the street, the tattoo shop had its lights off. But I bit my lower lip and imagined Myles still inside, wondering what he'd think if he saw me entering the same bar we met in. Not that I remember much of that night.

Originally, I hadn't planned to go out. But after class finished earlier today, Nellie suggested we get drinks and ogle pretty boys. And the bar did have some pretty boys to ogle.

Speaking of Nellie. I could see her seated in the back booth through the window. I laughed under my breath when I saw her still wearing her work uniform, which consisted of slacks and a loose, pastel pink blouse. She had an internship at some company doing marketing, which is why we ended up meeting at the bar instead of home. She probably got off from work recently, and since she worked near the strip, it made sense she come here right after.

Not that I dressed appropriate for the bar. I wore a black puffer jacket over my grey college sweater, but at least I dressed myself in straight jeans. I also applied some eye makeup and lifted my hair in a sleek ponytail. The effort was made.

It wasn't too cold tonight but either way, the walk wouldn't hurt. It only took ten minutes since I lived near the end of the strip, around the corner.

Taking my hand out from my pocket, I started to pull the door open when a feminine voice called out my name. Every bone in my body turned to stone while I stared forward.

"You're just going to ignore me?"

She was out of breath from the short jog she did to catch up to me, but I knew she wasn't tired. Valerie had a fit-girl lifestyle. At least from her social media page, she tried to act like it. She went to our school gym. She went on walks. She ran.

My roommate and friend was someone I idealized because of her intense work ethic. She was smart, took time for her physical health and even made time for numerous hobbies. And she filmed it all. Valerie Roche was someone girls looked up to, but not to me. Not anymore.

"Thea," she sighed, shuffling closer to me. "Remi told me you—"

"You spoke to him?"

I whirled my gaze to hers, surprised by the hostility in my tone. Even she seemed to reel her head back before she softened her gaze.

"Let me explain, okay? You can't keep on ignoring me. We have to talk about all this."

"We really don't, Val. You slept with my boyfriend. You don't get to act like you're the victim."

She looked horrified. "I know I'm not."

"Great. Then leave me alone." I didn't wait for her reply before I pulled the door open and stepped inside. But I didn't get far because next thing I knew, Valerie was shoving past me.

I stumbled for a moment. By the time my feet planted on the floor again, she blocked the second set of doors. In the dim lighting, I could still see how her eyes frantically watched me.

For a moment, I let myself be surprised because Val was actively contorting her face with emotion. Normally, she tries to keep her face smooth and wrinkle-free, but this desire wasn't anything new.

Valerie was Taiwanese but White on her dad's side. I've met her mother several times over the years, and while she was nice, I always heard her critiquing Val. Giving tips to keep her face looking young and fresh—which

I had to hand it to her, worked. Valerie porcelain skin glowed without a pimple or mole. No wrinkles around her eyes, nor her mouth.

When we first met, her dark brown hair fell close to her abdomen. Now it rested on her collarbone with blonde highlights—which didn't go well with her mother when she found out.

Her eyes were always something I loved. They were emerald green, and even though her eyes were small and slightly hooded, they always popped out when you looked at her. She had a snub nose that was always in the air. She hated it because her nostrils were visible, but considering she was five-three, hardly anyone could tell.

"We were drunk, okay?" She began, shakily lifting her hands in surrender. "And I know it's no excuse, but I thought you broke up, okay? It was his birthday and he was alone. He refused to talk about you, so I thought it was over."

I laughed hoarsely. "You're saying it's no excuse, but that's an excuse. Even if we did break up, there's a girl code, Val. You don't sleep with your friend's boyfriends. Or Ex's."

"I was drunk," she repeated, her eyes slightly narrowing in frustration. "You know how I get when I drink."

"You get impulsive. You don't sleep with someone's boyfriend!"

My voice was loud enough to get everyone's attention, even through the next set of doors. Valerie noticed and bleached in embarrassment before lowering her voice an octave.

"I'm sorry, okay? There's nothing I can do. I can't take it back. But we just have to move forward."

If I wasn't so angry, I would have laughed at her audacity. "If it were up to me, I'd kick you out."

Her eyes narrowed, but I felt proud of myself because I wasn't one for confrontation. Heck, I avoided conflict like it was a death sentence but right now, I didn't care if I hurt her feelings.

"You can't kick me out. I'm on the lease."

"Which is ending in June. Till then, stay away from me." With that, I walked to the side and narrowly missed slamming my shoulder into hers.

I kept my chin up as I walked the narrow pathway to the end of the bar. I spotted Nellie in the corner booth pressed against the window. The blinds were open and my steps faltered when I saw how busy the street was, even for a Thursday.

"Hey," I grumbled once I slipped into the seat opposite of Nellie. Since I faced the entrance, I gingerly lifted my head and sighed with relief when I saw Valerie nowhere to be found.

Nellie slammed her hand onto the table, bringing my attention back to her. "What the hell did she say to you?"

I pushed my shoulders back in preparation to rant, but my words came to a halt when my cell phone rang with a notification.

"Sorry," I breathed out, suddenly feeling exhausted while I lifted the phone toward me. My eyes bulged when I read the new message.

Who was that girl?

Myles saw me talking to Valerie? Was he in the bar?

Before I realized what I was doing, my head shot in all directions while simultaneously trying to spot the mountain of a man that was Myles. After a few seconds, my brows creased in confusion. He wasn't in the bar.

"What's wrong? It better not be bitch one and bitch two."

Her bitter tone made me grin for the first time tonight. "Bitch one and bitch two?"

She smirked slyly before sobering up. "Remi and Valerie. The freaking audacity they have. They hurt you, and if they cared about you at all, they should leave you alone." She sat up and cracked her knuckles. "Speaking of. What did the Satan say?"

"Is it Satan or bitch two?" I laughed, relaxing against the booth.

"Both. They're interchangeable, hun."

We shared a smile before she groaned. "Okay, so spill. What did the sea-witch say?"

"Three nicknames in a minute. New record," I teased, but Nellie kept her face impassive. The time for joking was over. I sighed and felt my cheeks losing colour as I thought back to my conversation with Valerie. There was an ache in my chest, but I ignored it.

The moment my lips parted, a familiar, gruff voice spoke up.

"I don't like being ignored."

Nellie and I snapped our head to the end of our booth, and I gaped when I saw Myles glaring at me heatedly. He wore dirty jeans with ink stains, and because his jacket was unzipped, I could see how his black shirt stretched across his hard chest.

When I flickered my gaze to his, my breath became shallow when I noted his tense posture. He lowered his chin more, not pulling his eyes off mine.

In the corner of my eye, I spotted Nellie shuffling uncomfortably in her seat but she didn't say anything—which shocked me.

I struggled to find my voice before I tightened my lips into a smile. "Seems like you should fix your expectations."

He inhaled sharply but said nothing else. When I turned to Nellie, she raised her brows with a silent question. I nodded shortly and her expression tightened before she stood up. "Okay. I'm going to... get us drinks."

I watched her go before hesitantly peeking at Myles. He never took his eyes off me, but I still sighed in relief when he moved to the spot Nellie occupied moments before.

When he didn't say anything, I took an encouraging breath.

"So," I dragged out slowly, "Twice in one day. That's a record."

He wore a blank expression, but his brow twitched for a millisecond before it returned to normal. Understanding what he wanted from me, I dramatically threw my head back and groaned. Although, it sounded more like I was choking.

"It's my roommate. The one who... you know." He didn't seem surprised by my admission. "But I think something's wrong with me because... I kind of feel bad."

At that, his eyebrows finally scrunched together. "Why would you feel bad?"

"I feel like I was too mean," I admitted shyly before cringing. "I like to think I'm not a rude person, but over the last week, I've felt so mean. Even though they deserve it. But I also refuse to be walked over, so I'm having a serious moral dilemma."

He almost looked amused. "There's no moral dilemma, princess. Give them shit. They fucking deserve it."

I smiled, but it was wobbly. "What are you doing here anyway? Do you typically stalk bars?"

"I don't drink, so no."

"You drank when we met." I pursed my lips in thought. "Or was I imagining that?"

He stiffened at the reminder of our first encounter. "That was a special occasion."

"Which was?"

Instead of answering right away, he lowered his head and smirked. "So many questions," he drawled, but he wasn't as irritated as last time. "I was getting off from work when I saw you talking to the girl. You didn't look good."

"How did I look?"

"Constipated."

I choked on a laugh while my cheeks flushed pink. "Gee. You really know how to compliment a woman." Mindlessly, I rubbed my cold hands over my cheeks before shrugging off my jacket. "You're only getting off work now? What time do you close?"

He sketched back against his seat. "Six-thirty today. But I needed to finish a tat."

"Oh." My eyes brightened before I brought my elbows to the table. I leaned forward and perched my chin into my hands. "What did you tattoo?"

Head tilted, he watched me with faint curiosity. "You want a tattoo or somethin'?" I lied and shook my head. He waited a few seconds before saying, "Tatted the dude's dog. Forearm."

"Do you have a picture?" For some reason, I was curious. I wanted to know how good Myles was at tattooing.

Wordlessly, he shoved a hand into his pocket and ripped out his phone. He pressed a few buttons before showing me the screen. My jaw hit the floor.

"You did that?" I rasped, not thinking as I took the phone from his hand. He didn't fight for it back, so I held it tighter while admiring the detailing of the tattoo. It was a front face portrait of a Rottweiler with floppy ears and for a moment, all I could to was stare in awe by how realistic it was. Almost as if it would hop out of the phone.

"You're so talented," I continued when he didn't say anything. "I wish I could draw with that."

"I don't draw," he said sharply. "It's a tattoo. Nothing else."

Surprised by the sudden anger lacing his tone, I lifted my head off his phone the same moment he snatched it from my grip.

I widened my eyes while the phone disappeared in his pocket again. I was about to ask what I did wrong when something sucked all the emotion out from his face. He broke the silence first.

"You never answered my question."

"You asked me a question?" My brows knitted, trying to recall our conversation. "What did you ask?"

"Not now. When I texted you earlier."

Again, I was going to ask what he meant when memories slammed back into me. Memories from class today. Or more specifically, his question that I adamantly avoided responding to. My sex list.

His brow rose when I didn't say anything, so I tightened my thighs and locked my ankles together to stop myself from fidgeting.

"Well," I coughed before surveying the busy bar, only to sigh in relief when I saw Nellie flirting with the bartender. "I think I need alcohol before I can answer that question."

"I have all day. Maybe when friend returns with your drinks, you'll tell her—"

I didn't think as I threw myself over the table, slapping a hand over his mouth. My eyes bulged nervously at the thought of Nellie knowing about the list, and this shithead must have known that. I felt his mouth pulling into a smirk underneath my hand.

"Not one word, Myles. Not one word."

He lingered his focus on me before he nodded once. Only then did I peel away from him. I tried to fight my embarrassment over this situation—a situation I basically put myself in. Myles never turned his eyes away from me while I pulled the small notebook out of my jacket pocket. And I do mean small. It was four-by-six inches.

For the first time since he sat down, his eyes shined with unrestrained amusement.

"Is that what I think it is?"

I pouted and brought the notebook to my chest. "No judgments."

"No judging here," he replied deeply, but I didn't miss how his mouth quirked. "You wrote your list down?"

"Well... it's more satisfying to cross things out when it's written."

He considered me silently. "Does that mean you plan on crossing things out from the list?"

"Now who's asking a bunch of questions," I snapped, but I failed at sounding intimidating because Myles only smiled wider—at least, wider in his category. The other side of his mouth lifted slightly.

"Can I see it?" He drawled lowly, and apparently I wanted to die of humiliation because I gave it to him.

The only comforting thought I had was that he already knew about the list and still hasn't run away. Not that I would ever blame him. I would run away from me.

Suddenly feeling anxious, I laced my fingers and watched as his eyes travelled over the first page. After a few seconds, he started to smirk.

"Boyfriend never fucked you in the shower, princess?"

"Can it, batman."

He tensed before his eyes shot to mine. I read the question in his gaze before smiling proudly. "Well, it's only fair to call you batman if you persist on calling me princess. By the way, not all of Disney's movies have princesses."

"Sure, princess." He went back to reading my list. I tried to stop my frown from growing while he flipped to the next page. He laughed under his breath after a while, and it felt like a punch to my throat. "Some of these are serious BDSM shit. You wouldn't like it."

His tone wasn't accusatory, but I still narrowed my eyes. "How would you know what I would or wouldn't like? You've only known me a week."

"Ten days, sweetheart." He lifted his head and ignored my glare before raising an expected brow. "And I don't need to know who you are. I know what girls like you like."

"Girls like me? Careful, Myles. It sounds like you're about to generalize."

"Girls like you want a prince charming. Want the flowers, the gifts. You want love comin' at you at face-value. You want a happily ever after."

He said the words so bitterly, it made me frown. "You make it sound like I'm shallow." His lips pursed, but I cut him off before he could say anything else. "And who doesn't want to have a happily ever after? Who doesn't want to live a happy life?"

"It's not about want, princess. It's about being realistic. That shit only exists in the movies. And this," he brought the list up, "Isn't realistic. How do you plan on crossing this shit out? You gonna walk up to someone and ask them to fuck you outside?"

I cringed at his harsh tone, but I was thankful he spoke in a low hiss. It didn't seem like anybody heard.

"Well, I was considering to go to a sex club—"

"A sex club?" He was seething now, but I think he realized he was showing too much emotion because he sat back and aggressively rubbed his face in frustration. "Jesus fucking Christ, girl. You wanna know what kinda fucked up men go there? You wanna put yourself in that situation?"

"What are you suggesting, Myles? Are you going to help me get laid?" I said louder than intended. The people in the booth in front of me turned around and watched me with furrowed brows. The group of guys in the circular table a few feet to my right eyed with interest.

I slapped myself in the face and groaned. "Kill me."

"Whattt did I walk into," Nellie said, stopping at the foot of the booth. I wanted to bang my face on the table. The only reason I stopped myself was because she lowered our drinks onto the surface and I didn't want to spill the liquid gold.

Myles didn't say anything. Begrudgingly, I lifted my eyes to his—which were already laser focused on me. Next thing I knew, his hand slid underneath the table and handed me the notebook so Nellie wouldn't see. I smiled appreciatively before he stood up and exited the booth.

"I'll be in touch." With a parting nod, he stalked toward the exit without looking back.

It wasn't until he was outside and out from hearing range did Nellie plop onto her seat across from me. "Who the hell was that?"

"That's Myles." I was struggling to form sentences let alone lie, so I decided to go with the truth. "We met here that night. He helped me get home."

Her nose flared in disgust before sliding one of the glasses to me. "What were you saying about getting laid? Are you planning to sleep with him?"

I scoffed, but my cheeks brightened tomato red. "No. No. I was just saying how I was... considering to have a rebound. Not with him," I hurriedly added. "With someone else."

The thought of mentioning an actual sex list to Nellie had me revolting in fear. She could never know. Fortunately, I was a decent liar because she eyed me in consideration before slowly sagging in her seat. "Okay. Good. That's good."

"That's good?" I wasn't expecting that reaction, let alone the smile she sent me seconds later.

"You should sleep with someone. Preferably someone you already know. Who won't take advantage of you. You're still vulnerable."

I nodded quickly in agreement while she continued to offer me advice. Safety types. All while her motherly speech, I couldn't help but feel sick of myself because I wanted to be taken advantage of. I didn't want vulnerable, safe sex. I wanted the opposite of Remi—opposite of all the guys I've slept with before him. But what did that say about me? What did that say about my character?

God. What would Nellie say?

"Let's cheers," she chirped, and I blinked back to reality as she lifted her glass. "To new beginnings."

Weakly, I brought my glass to hers. "And better futures."

We clinked our cups together, but while she took a few sips, I drank half of it in seconds. To new possibilities.

□□□·□ □·□□□

happy Friday everyone! Cool news for me, not so much for you: by the time I update next week, I'll be done exams ;)

I'll leave you with that because I'm drowning in cue cards, have a happy weekend xx

Chapter 5

CHAPTER VWingman

□□□·□ □·□□□

"Are you sure you don't want me to come with you?" My best friend fumbled with the hem of her shirt while a pained grimace swept across her face. Nellie's been watching me pace frantically for the last five minutes.

Forcing my feet to park in front of her, I curled my toes and smiled—although, it felt like I was fighting the urge to vomit. "I'm okay. Honestly. Plus, you wouldn't want to come with me anyways. I'm meeting Myles."

Her nose scrunched in disgust before quickly sobering. I knew she didn't like Myles. I could pretend that it was because of how he acts, but I knew she was judging him based on his looks.

I've tried defending his honour. She'd nod. Smile faintly. But her eyes always squinted in disbelief before it'd go away. I couldn't be upset with her, though. She was coming from a good place, and I expected her to be wary. As an older sister to her siblings, Nellie always had her eye out for possible danger, which made her alert. And as much as she tried to hide it from me, I knew she was wary with Myles.

"Just Myles?" She asked hesitantly, still leaning against my door frame. When I nodded, she breathed in. "Okay, well... just keep me updated. And I mean every hour."

"Yes mother," I teased, but that only made her pout.

"You can't blame me for worrying. This guy... I don't know, hun. You just met him and—"

"We've been talking almost every day for the last two weeks," I told her, not that she didn't already know.

Last I saw him, he caught me at the bar with Nellie. When I got home a few hours later, I froze when I saw a missed message from him, asking how my night went. Next thing I knew, we were aimlessly talking about the most random stuff until two in the morning. Neither of us made an effort to meet up with one another, not that I was desperate to see him. I had three midterms last week, so studying took up most of my energy.

Granted, I didn't have an excuse for this week. I spent my reading week either writing term papers, submitting articles to the newsletter or drinking with Nellie. At least I could end my Friday with a bang. Literally. Hopefully.

Myles, the trooper he was, didn't want me to spread my legs to the first guy who gave me attention. He told me to be patient, and normally, I was a patient person. But after writing down my sex list, I realized the competitive streak I had—with myself. I wanted to check things off the list. My fingers were twitching.

When we were texting two nights ago, I told him I wanted sex—not with him, obviously. The text bubbles appeared and disappeared for a solid thirty seconds and I smiled, imagining him gaping at his phone. Unfortunately for me, I have yet to see him display a full face of actual emotion.

"I just feel like he's using you for sex," Nellie's troubled sigh took me out from my thoughts. I fought a smirk.

Au contraire, Nellie. I'm using him for sex. Well, sex advice. Same thing.

"You told me it was a good idea to rebound," I reminded her, even though I knew it would never happen. With Myles, at least. Otherwise he would have offered to "help me" with his penis, not his wingman abilities.

"Rebounds are supposed to happen in one night. One and done. And you told me you weren't going to do it with him." She paused, her eyes widening in fear. "Wait, are you dating him? Crap, Allie. I thought you weren't ready after what happened with Remi. I don't know if Myles is a good choice. He doesn't even look like he considers having a girlfriend—"

My laughter stopped her from ranting more. "He's teaching me how to drink more responsibly," I lied to ease her fears. If she knew I was actively looking for sex with—gasp—a stranger, she'd faint. Probably before handing me a safe-sex pamphlet and giving me a lecture about stranger danger.

I'm not completely oblivious to the horrors most women go through. If a woman hasn't been sexually assaulted, she more than likely knows someone who has.

For us, it was Valerie. It happened when she was a freshman, and she'd been so scarred that she only slept with women until two years ago. Another reason why I'm surprised she slept with Remi.

Nellie's snort dragged me out from my dark thoughts. "You? Drink responsibly? You literally took two shots of vodka before you started getting ready."

"Liquor courage," I said defensively. "I need liquor courage."

"Yes, and two shots will work so well. I can tell by how much you were pacing."

"I paced so the alcohol could run through my body quicker." I grinned in satisfaction. "It did."

Nellie rolled her eyes but fought a smile while pushing herself off the door frame. She stepped into the hall but gave me a lingering look before deadpanning, "You better keep me updated or I'll call the cops on your ass."

I blew her a kiss. "I'll be responsible."

"Promise?"

"I'll try to be responsible," I rephrased with a blinding smile. Nellie didn't look phased.

She turned her back to me and walked away, but not before grumbling under her breath, "I'm losing years of my life because of you."

"Love you," I shouted, cupping my mouth. She made a disbelieving grunt before she closed her bedroom door.

Wearing a faint smile, I moved around my room to prepare my purse before deciding last minute that I wouldn't bring one. I also needed my outfit to look good, I scarified warmth.

Because I had to acknowledge my curves, I wore a spaghetti strap, ruched and velvet wine red dress that hugged my body. I didn't wish for death, though, so I slipped into my worn-out ankle boots. While I liked heels, walking ten minutes in them, plus in the winter? Not for me. I like my ankles.

Even though my long hair already had some shape, I still curled it into subtle beach curls. My face wasn't necessarily caked with makeup, but it was still a full face. I smiled in relief when my eyeliner came out better than expected.

We were meeting at the club for nine, so I needed to leave within the next few minutes. However, as I was slipping into my loosely fitted leather jacket, my phone started ringing.

I unplugged it from its charger, only to choke on saliva when I saw who was calling me. Who has never called me, even after two weeks of texting.

Internally freaking out, I almost dropped the phone but I managed to juggle it back up before answering the call out of breath. "Hello?"

There was a short pause on the other line, followed by a short, gruff laugh. "You good, princess?"

"What do you mean?" My voice hit a new pitch. I hurriedly cleared my throat before continuing, "I'm fine. Why wouldn't I be fine?"

"I wouldn't know the answer to that," he drawled blankly, but I couldn't help but feel he was sarcastic.

"Are you implying I'm not fine?"

He didn't respond right away. "Princess, I'm taking you to the club to practice your flirting so you can get laid."

"Are you judging a woman for wanting sex?" I accused, narrowing my eyes at my own reflection. "You don't have to come—"

"I never said that," he cut me off soberly. "You're putting words into my mouth. I'm just saying this is risky."

"Riskier than me going to a sex club?" I smiled when I heard him snarl warningly.

"You're not going to a fucking sex club. Get it out of your mind already."

I laughed. "I'm joking. God, batman. Lighten up."

He grumbled something under his breath. It sounded like I can't believe I'm doing this.

I only smiled wider. "So, what's up? Why'd you call?"

Realizing that I was giving him the opportunity to change the topic, he said roughly, "You good if I pick you up?"

"Are you sure?" I swear I could hear him grinding his teeth. "If it's not out of the way for you?"

"It's not," he asserted dryly. "I'll be there in a minute."

"Wait, you don't know my—" he hung up before I could finish. "Address."

For a moment, I stood in the centre of my room with a mixture of disbelief and confusion before remembering what he said. He'd be here in a minute.

Running around my room hysterically, I searched for my ID before shoving it behind my phone case. The stupid jacket had stupidly small pockets that could barely fit anything. Stupidly.

At least it could fit my phone, albeit barely.

Already dressed in my shoes, I ran to the opposite side of the house and shouted, "I'm leaving! Lock the door!" Before thrusting myself outside.

By the time I jogged down the several porch steps and paused by the curb, I realized Myles still hadn't arrived. I was out of breath for nothing.

Even though the air was cold, it wasn't windy—either way, I didn't mind. I've walked to a club in all types of weather conditions in the last three-ish years.

Casually, I tilted my head to the street on my right, which led to the strip, and I furrowed my brows when a motorcycle revved its engine. Not a second later, it spun onto my side of the street. I jumped back when it screeched into a stop in front of me.

Because the driver wasn't wearing a helmet, I stomped toward the motorcycle and slapped his arm. "Why aren't you wearing protective gear?" I demanded, but clearly I didn't sound demanding enough because Myles' mouth twitched in a smirk before he threw his leg off his ride.

Even though my boots had a heel in them, the moment Myles straightened, he was towering over me. I couldn't help but feel overwhelmed for a second before pinching my lips together.

"The helmet would be for you, princess."

"Well, you could wear the helmet before you picked me up." I shook my head in disbelief before looking at the bike. Feeling amused, I chuckled. "I'm not sure why I feel surprised that you drive a motorcycle. You seem like the type."

Even in the dark, I could tell it was an older model. Though, it did seem well kept.

"What, princess? Guys in your Disney movies don't drive motorcycles?"

I cracked a smile before tsking playfully. "More like horses, but nobody's perfect."

When our eyes met, he smirked a little wider. That was, until his eyes fell to my dress.

"Fucks sake, girl. It's freezing out and you're wearing that?" He scolded harshly, but I didn't miss how his eyes kept on lingering on my legs.

I waved his worries away. "I'm used to walking in the cold. Most girls know the scarifies." Then, I gestured to him. "And look who's talking. That jacket keeping you warm?"

"Warmer than whatever the hell you're wearing." His dark eyes were still peering over my body, and for some reason, it made my heart flip with anxiety. Do I not look good?

"You look fucking good, Althea. Get the thought out of your head," he gritted out almost angrily. It took me a moment to realize that I spoke out loud. "You're going to get cold."

"Well, that won't be our only problem, then." When he finally lifted his eyes to mine, clearly confused, I nodded to his motorcycle. "I'm gonna get you solve a fun math equation."

His expression turned sour. It took a lot of strength not to laugh. "Motorcycle plus wearing a dress equals...." When he didn't answer, I clapped my hands and exclaimed, "Everyone seeing the goodies!"

Clearly unhappy with that realization, he glared. "You can meet me there, Myles. It's okay," I offered with a small smile. "I have no problems walking. Honest."

He continued glaring. I was starting to understand that this was his thinking face.

I cocked my head and smiled at him with amusement until suddenly, he kicked himself off the curb and toward his motorcycle. I figured he was accepting my Get Out of Jail Free card because he hopped over his ride and jerked it with a start, but he only surprised me instead.

Jaw slack, I watched as he manoeuvred his motorcycle onto my driveway before turning it off with a huff.

"Myles, you don't have to—"

"Shut it, princess."

He strode toward me with a dark expression which would normally get me running in the opposite direction. Instead, I stayed locked in my spot while he shrugged his jacket off and threw it over my shoulders impatiently.

"Let's go." He was already striding across the street while I gaped at his departing back.

Cursing under my breath, I broke out into a short jog before catching up to him. "Myles, take your jacket. You're going to get cold."

He snorted, and I felt like I wasn't in on a joke. "Cold doesn't affect me, princess. Keep the jacket."

Knowing that I wasn't going to win this argument with him, I begrudgingly slipped my arms into the sleeves. He didn't look at me once, so I mumbled a soft, "Thank you."

"Don't mention it. Literally."

"What? You trying to keep a bad guy persona, batman?"

"Told you you're my New Year's resolution. Nobody else."

"Again with the resolution." I smiled and fastened my pace when his strides became longer. He must have noticed because after a moment, he slowed down. "So tell me. What spurred on this wish to be nice? Were you on the naughty list last Christmas?"

My tease wasn't met with a smile. If anything, more lines creased his forehead as he glowered.

"So why doesn't the cold effect you?" I asked instead, but he still didn't answer. He was avidly avoiding eye contact, and I realized he was building walls. Then I remembered I was asking too many questions. After scolding myself, I put a skip in my step and smiled. "The cold doesn't bother me much either. I actually like it. Most of the times, at least. My ears get really cold, and yeah my hair can keep it warm but that doesn't usually help because the wind pushes it away."

I breathed in through my teeth and fixed my hair over my ears. "Like right now." I didn't bother giving him the chance to talk, I was full on rambling now and no one could stop me. "Anyway, I think I'm more warm-blooded cause my parents are from Greece. Well, my mom is. She was actually born there. My dad is Greek too, but he was born in the States. Did I ever mention how they met?"

"They're actually the reason why I believe in happily ever afters," I rushed out, not realizing how much I was talking with my hands. "My mom was in her first year studying Greek mythology in university. My dad was travelling around Europe before he decided to visit the place his ancestors were from. They met at a coffee shop, how cute is that?"

"I was an accident though," it came out with a laugh, but something in my chest squeezed with painful memories I'd like to keep repressed.

Gaze trained to the pavement. I briefly noted how much we slowed down, but that realization was quickly drowned out by the feeling of Myles' eyes on me.

Exhaling shakily, I admired the fog leaving my lips before tipping my head toward Myles. I was right: he was watching me.

I forced a smile. "They're travelling now. No idea where they are though. Probably somewhere in Asia."

He studied me silently for a moment. Lights filled the street, either from hanging lanterns or post lights and yet, I couldn't tell what his eyes were glinting with.

"No siblings?" He shocked me by asking. So much so that I couldn't stop myself from scoffing, much harsher than intended.

"Ah, no." I tried to lighten my tone by laughing. "But I'm good at sharing! What about you? Brother? Sister?"

Apparently that was too personal to the man because yet again, he didn't reply. Before I could frown and ask him what was wrong, he stopped walking suddenly.

My feet faltered as I twisted my gaze forward, only to gasp in a last-second realization that I was about to bump into someone. Before the collision happened, there was a strong grip on my elbow before I was tugged back into a hard chest. It took me a few seconds to recognize that it was Myles that stopped me from making an utter fool of myself.

"Thanks." I fought a blush as I treaded backwards just enough so there was space between us.

He nodded once in acknowledgement, so I took the moment to check out our surroundings. There was a line of people waiting to enter the club, and because it was a Friday night, the line was long. Probably a thirty-minute wait.

I glanced to Myles and my eyebrows furrowed when I caught him observing our environment. No, observing wasn't the right word. Scrutinizing. As if he was searching for something in specific.

"So..." His spine stiffened, so I took that as a good sign that he wasn't completely ignoring me. "What's the plan, batman? Also, before we do anything, I'll probably need a shot. Or several. I pre-drank before I left but I think the walk kinda sobered me up. Sadly."

His eyes focused on the groups of people walking all over the busy street before, finally, he lowered his chin and turned to me.

"You do want to do this, right? You're not regretting this?"

His hazel eyes were abnormally dark now. Still, his head shook no. "I'm not regretting anything. Just thinking."

"About what? You're not considering to throw me into the wolves, right?"

I felt a wave of relief when his lip curled into a small smirk. "No, princess. No wolves today." He jerked his head to the club entrance. "When we get in there, though, you're going to show me what you're made of."

My entire face contorted in a wince. "That's not a good idea, I promise. My flirting... it's bad. Like worse than bad. I swear, even before I started dating Remi, I could hardly handle a conversation with a guy without joking about something. Something way too inappropriate to say with a stranger."

His eyes gleamed with a mixture of amusement and wickedness. "Any examples?"

"You're probably going to want to stop associating with me after I tell you." He gave me a bored look. I sighed and peered to the light behind him, so I wouldn't see his judgment. Or laughter. "Senior year, this guy on the football team tried talking to me. I was a nervous wreck because he was just staring at me. Or more specifically, my boobs. I tried making conversation and every time I opened my mouth, it felt like word vomit. Next thing I knew, I tried talking about football and then I..."

I flattened my palm over my face, wishing I could slap the memory out of my brain. "Then I asked if he liked to play with balls. And when he said nothing, I asked if he prefers smaller balls or bigger balls. Then I said, 'you must like big balls because you play football.' To say I was the laughingstock of the century that year is putting it lightly, Myles."

For a long, long moment, I kept my gaze screwed onto the post light. But when Myles didn't say anything, I forced myself to take a small peek in his direction.

My heart stammered in my chest from what I saw.

Myles had his eyes wide while curling his lips inward, as if he was struggling to keep back a laugh. The moment his eyes met mine, that's when it happened.

Myles freaking laughed.

Not just a small chuckle like the other times. He did a whole ass, chest rumbling, eyes crinkling laugh. And for some reason, all my embarrassment and stress evaporated because I made Myles laugh. I watched him try to sober up in amazement.

"Princess, I..." He choked on a chuckle before shaking his head. "That is fucking ridiculous, but I wouldn't expect any less from you and that mouth of yours."

I tried to prevent myself from smiling, but it crept out. "Alright, so next time I tell you to shut me up before my rambling gets worse, do it."

"Oh I'm never doing that now," he scoffed. "I wanna see what else you come up with."

He responded to my glare with a smirk before patting his chest. "Do your worst."

My brows knitted. "What do you mean?"

"Flirt with me, princess. I know you want to."

I wanted to argue that no, I didn't. But Myles watched me cockily, as if he expected I'd back out, and that only stroked my recently developed competitive side.

Without thinking, I lifted my hand and gently touched his bicep. I didn't know what I was expecting from the physical contact, but I definitely didn't expect to feel goosebumps rising on my arm—and I couldn't even blame it on the cold because I was wearing two jackets.

Myles wasn't wearing a jacket, and yet, I could feel the heat flooding out from his body and onto my hand. I tried not to focus on how I could barely wrap my fingers around half of his arm. And I especially tried not to focus on how solid he was built.

"You have... nice bones," I tried to compliment, but it came out more like a question. When his mouth started lifting into a smirk, I shoved his arm away from me. "Why do I even bother?"

"That's a start," he tried to offer encouragingly, but my lips only pursed together. He exhaled while his eyes roamed over me in thought. "Words are one thing, princess. But you also gotta look like you mean it."

"What's that supposed to mean?"

"Well, you tried complimenting my arms but you looked ready to throw up."

"I did not!"

He smirked knowingly. "Did to." Before I could defend myself, the words died in my throat when suddenly, Myles was holding the side of my head with his large hand. My eyes blurred in surprise before he began rubbing his thumb in soothing circles on my forehead.

"Gotta relax these muscles, princess," he murmured while watching his hand remain on my face. "Need to look like you enjoy flirting. If you wanna sleep with someone, you gotta look like you want it."

I kept lingering on his contemplative expression before he finally met my gaze. His hand reluctantly fell away from my face once my wrinkles smoothed out.

"And if I flirt, that means I want it?"

"Not all the time, but it's a good sign."

I watched him silently for a moment before tilting my head in a small smile. "I like your smile. It's very Disney when you don't try to hide it."

His eyes shot to mine, but if he was surprised he didn't show it.

"Good?" I asked with a quirked brow.

A long pause before he grunted, "Good."

Using the silence to check out our surroundings, I noticed we were getting closer to the front door. Less than a dozen people left.

"Has Remi tried to talk to you since that day?" His question jolted me back, but he kept his expression impassive.

I found my voice after a second. "Sometimes, yeah. Last time I saw him was on Thursday. He was waiting outside after one of my classes, but I had Nellie with me. She told him off." I smiled at the memory before shaking my head. "A few days ago he dropped off flowers."

"Flowers?"

"Yeah." I tightened my lips before sighing in defeat. "I don't have anything against them. I think they're really pretty, but they're also too high maintenance. Plus they die quick. I would love to own a plant. Not right now, though, cause I'd probably kill it."

"So what would you have right now? Instead of flowers."

"Probably pencil crayons," I admitted sheepishly and rocked back on my heels. "I like to draw in one of those stress-free colouring books when I have time. I bought one with a cottage core theme in the beginning of the year, so it helps me fulfill my desire to own a plant at the moment."

"It's funny, though. Val thought the flowers were for her. She swears it's because of an admirer she has, not because she assumes Remi would send her flowers, but what do I know." I shrugged to hide the ache in my chest. Even though it's been weeks, their betrayal feels like I got violently stabbed.

I felt Myles' gaze on me. "Is he stalking you?" When I shrugged again, I swear I could hear him gritting his teeth before he bit out, "Gimme your phone, princess."

Confused and curious, I handed him my phone slowly. The moment it was close enough, he snatched it out from my grip and demanded the password. I gave it to him and watched with growing amusement as he tried to manoeuvre my phone—or specifically, my home page.

"Do you need he—"

"No." He pressed on the text message icon and my heart leapt up my throat.

"Myles, don't even think about texting him."

"I'm not," he grumbled before finding his contact. His thumb hovered for a moment, though, and I was about to ask what was wrong when I realized he was staring at his contact name. It wasn't anything creative: just a bat emoji next to his nickname, batman.

Finally, he pressed his contact a little harder than necessary. He pressed a few buttons until suddenly, he was scrolling through my photos.

"What are you doing?" I gasped, lurching for my phone. He easily dodged my advances while using his other arm to keep me away. "Myles! You don't go through a girl's photos! It's private!"

"There's so many fucking screenshots," he muttered gruffly before his fingers finally stopped scrolling. I threw my head back in surprise when I saw that he pulled up my schedule—which I took a picture of at the start of the year. "Finally."

I watched in disbelief as he sent my schedule to himself. I continued staring at him that way until he locked my phone and handed it back to me. He cocked his head in confusion when he noticed. "What?"

"What?" I repeated, dumbfounded. "What will you do with that information?"

"Make sure your fucking ex isn't stalking you, that's one."

I frowned even though I felt somewhat awed by his statement. "You don't have to worry about me, Myles."

Unfortunately for me, we finally reached the beginning of the line so he didn't end up gracing me with a reply. The female bouncer barely tapped my body while the male bouncer went a little too aggressive on Myles. I glared, but just as I opened my mouth to call him out, he finished and Myles walked in my direction.

He noticed my furious expression and said nothing, but he tilted his body closer to me. I wasn't sure if he'd done that on purpose, but I didn't pull away from him instantly.

Thankfully, the first place he led us to was the bar, where I graciously took three shots while Myles watched. The moment I started feeling tipsy, I gave him a toothy grin and a thumbs up, which he responded with a shake of his head.

For a few minutes, he gave me a few pointers—or warnings—on how to initiate a dance with a guy who won't take advantage. I barely let him finish before I basically hurled myself onto the dance floor. It wasn't long until I found a dance partner, and when I thought Myles had completely abandoned me and left me to fend for myself, I peered toward the bar.

And there he was. Watching, like always.

For a moment, I let my drunk thoughts take over because as I grinded on the guy behind me, I couldn't help but consider: what if he helped me?

□□□·□ □·□□□

EXAMS ARE DONE !! but I have a major headache and migraine so did I really win? :')

I've been away from home for three weeks, and tomorrow, I will finally be a nuisance to them again (wish me luck with packing)

nonetheless, I hope you enjoyed the chapter, hopefully next Friday will be better x

Chapter 6

- -

CHAPTER VIToy Story

□□□·□ □·□□□

Whoever said to take two, three hour lectures in one day needs a place in hell. I wasn't sure if I was in the right mind when I made my schedule, but if I could talk to my old self—the one from two months ago—I would scream 'do not take two classes back-to-back on Tuesday's!'

Although, I did have to hand it to my media ethics professor. He let us out of class an hour early.

So here I am, skipping gladly on the sidewalk with a smile at five in the evening. The distance between school and the house took fifteen minutes, so as I strutted through the busy strip, I plugged in my earbuds and searched for my big-dick energy playlist when I got an idea.

Lifting my head away from my phone, I glanced around the street before my eyes fell to the tattoo shop across from me. Even though my body was exhausted and deprived of sleep, next thing I knew, I was opening another app and texting Myles.

How much money would it take for you to watch a movie with me?

I slowed my pace while waiting for his reply. It same less than a minute later.

What movie?

Grinning wickedly I frenziedly typed, Disney. Maybe Pixar.

The message sent, and three dots appeared. Then disappeared. His stunned silence brought me to the brink of laughter, but my smile shattered when my phone lit up with his name printed across the screen.

I choked on saliva the same moment I nearly fell on my own feet. Luckily, I managed to stabilize myself before answering the call. "Walt Disney Studios speaking."

"Funny." His voice was clipped, making me frown. "We aren't watching that shit, princess."

Even though he offended the creator of my favourite movies, my eyes widened in shock and eagerness. "Does that mean you do want to watch a movie? I should warn you though, I'm tired as hell. I'll probably pass out, but then again, you're probably tired too, right? I know you mentioned that you finish work at six-thirty so that means you must have been working for eight hours? Wait, what time do you start working? Did you ever tell me? I don't think you're an early bird. You seem like you..."

His silence reminded me that I've been rambling for over a minute now. I felt my face burning red in embarrassment. "Please shut me up."

"Why would I do that?" I could hear the small smirk in his voice. "I just got five dollars for the question jar."

"We're not actually doing that!"

"Scared you gonna be broke, princess?"

"Look who's asking questions now," I grumbled in frustration.

There was a moment of silence. "I start at one. Sometimes I take in earlier clients."

His admission made my lip twitch. "Does that mean you want to come over? I don't think I have to let you know where I live." More questions filtered through my brain, and I debated on asking where he lived.

"I'm still at work," he deadpanned coolly. My forehead puckered at his impassive tone, but it smoothed out when he added, "I can be there for seven."

"Perfect! Gives me enough time to shower and eat. Wait, do you want to eat too? I can order us something—"

"Fuck's sake, princess. You don't need to do all that."

"I know I don't need to. But I was taught to be a good host—"

"Don't host with me, sweetheart. Not worth the effort."

"So... you don't want food?"

"I'm good."

Something shifted in his tone. It almost felt as if he was closing his walls around him—walls I was getting all too familiar with. Considering that I've known the brute for a month, I'm getting used to his savage remarks and uncaring stares. Yet, every time he tries to wiggle away from me—as if he's scared to get to close—I feel his hesitation. In those moments, I try to see if I could psychoanalyze him.

Considering the only psychology I know is from my first year, introduction to psychology class, it hardly works. I wouldn't be surprised if he's used to pushing people away, though. The man's confessed he has no friends, and for some reason, it makes me feel sympathetic. It makes me want to be his first friend.

My drifting thoughts halted when my phone rang against my ear. Checking the contact, I cursed loud enough for Myles to hear.

"What?" He bit out almost instantly. I thought he was mad at me at first, but then he clenched out, "What happened, Althea?"

"N-no, it's nothing. It's my mom." I wanted to smack myself in the face. Get it together, Thea. "She's calling me. Talk later?"

The moment he grunted in agreement, I ended the call and answered mom's. "Hey mom!" I squeaked nervously before clearing my throat. "How are you? You're awake?"

"It's only eleven-thirty, sweetie," she chirped happily. I faintly heard the sound of music playing in the background. "Your father and I are taking advantage of the night. Switzerland is wonderful."

"Oh, you're back in Europe?"

"Yes, yes. We finished jumping around Asia, but I convinced your dad to extend our trip. I wanted to see some more places before we settle back to Detroit." Her voice was wistful, and it made my chest pang because I knew the only reason they waited until now to travel was because of me.

Because they didn't want me.

I drowned those harmful thoughts away, but my steps pounded the sidewalk a little harder.

"—is school?" I managed to catch the end of mom's sentence before cringing.

"Sorry, mom. What was that?" I tried to control my blush as I turned the corner to my street.

"How is school?" She repeated before hesitantly saying, "How's Remi?"

I stopped walking and clenched the phone tighter because I knew my mom. And she wouldn't ask about Remi unless she knew something. "What do you know?"

It took a few moments before she sighed in defeat. "Well, I spoke to Lillian, and she said that Remi told her you wanted a break. That you were too stressed to deal with a relationship. Did something happen, Thea?"

"He... he said that?" I gritted my teeth so hard I felt like they were seconds away from chipping. "He said I wanted a break?"

Her response came cautiously. "I'm guessing that was a lie?"

"He cheated on me, mom," I said sharply, uncaring that I blew Remi's attempt to keep everything hushed. "With Val, my roommate. He cheated a month ago."

"Wha—a month?" She gasped. She must have moved away from wherever she was because the music seemingly disappeared. "Remi cheated on you? He loves you. Why would he do that?"

I knew she was asking herself that question. I answered it for her anyways. "He says it happened because he was drunk and lonely. I think he was angry. Maybe he didn't think about it this way, but I feel like he wanted to get back at me."

"Why was he angry at you?"

Sighing, I gave a quick rundown of what happened the night of Remi's birthday. When I finished, mom let out an exasperated breath. "When Lillian finds out, she'll kill him. I can't believe he lied."

I wanted to say I was surprised too, but I couldn't. For our entire lives, Remi tried to be the best he could. The best student. The best son. The best friend. The best boyfriend. It's like he needed to prove to everyone he was a good guy. So, it's not alarming that he lied—especially so he could keep his good boy persona to his adoptive parents.

"I'm sorry, darling." It felt like mom's soothing voice cradled me to her chest. In that moment, my eyes burned with unshed tears. "Why didn't you tell me as soon as it happened?"

I smiled wobbly and continued walking the rest of the short distance to my house. "You're on vacation. I didn't want to bother you." I didn't think you'd care.

Angrily, I repressed those thoughts with a sharp shake of my head. "Anyway, don't tell Lillian. I have to call her soon anyways. About the internship I probably won't get because of Remi."

Thankfully, she didn't notice my desperation to change the topic. "Why would you think that? She'd love for you to work at the magazine. And she isn't responsible for who gets the internships. You will wow them all by yourself."

Suddenly, someone called out her name. I recognized my dad's gruff voice. "Darling, I have to go. We're at this little nightclub and it's getting chilly outside. Let me know when you talk to her, okay? I'll call you tomorrow."

"Okay. Bye mo—" Before I could finish, she hung up.

I exhaled slowly before shoving my phone back into my jacket. I contemplated on playing music, but I was already crossing the street and walking toward the bungalow. I used my time to consider what I would eat now that I'm home. I brought a few snacks to my classes, but I didn't have time to have lunch, so I haven't eaten since breakfast.

The moment my feet hit the porch steps, I lifted my head and scrutinized the stairs to make sure there wasn't any black ice laying around. My body turned rigid a few moments later when I spotted someone sitting on the top of the stairs, watching me intently.

It took me a second to find my voice. When I did, I squeezed the straps of my school bag. "What are you doing here?"

Remi flinched from my hostile tone. "Come on, Thea. I'm giving you your space, but I miss you. I said I'm sorry—"

"No, you didn't." He frowned in confusion, so I stated slowly, "You never apologized. Not that it would matter. We're done, Remi."

For a few, dragging moments, he watched me almost in disbelief. The realization that he never apologized shocked him. "Okay, then let me say it now. I'm sorry."

I couldn't help it. I smiled sadly. "Say I take you back. What would that say about me? About how much I value myself? Do you think that little of me?"

"Of course not," he rushed in frustration before walking down a few steps. He kept a respectful distance between us. "This isn't about your self-worth, Thea. This is... this is about you giving me a second chance. I messed up, I know that. But we can get past this. We can get through anything."

His softened chestnut eyes brought me back to all those times he tried convincing me of doing things I didn't want to do. Going to a party hosted by my former bully. Drinking with said bully. Making sure I didn't show off my boobs too much. And it worked. Every. Single. Time.

Maybe I was easy to manipulate. Maybe I looked for the good so much that I was blind to the bad. But looking at Remi now, knowing what he's done? It's the nail in the coffin. There's no going back.

He moved down another stair slowly, as if he was worried if he moved too fast, he'd scare me away. "Maybe we can grab coffee," he offered gently with a crooked smile. "Talk. Catch up. I miss you."

Next thing I knew, Remi's hand cupped my cheek. His thumb barely grazed my mouth before I snapped my head away from him.

"Don't," I barked and shouldered passed him in fury. My keys were already out of my pocket and in my hands when I reached the front door. The moment I shoved the key inside the lock, Remi flattened his hand on the door, keeping me from pulling it open. I resisted a shiver when I felt him breathing down my neck. I wasn't sure if it was from disgust or nostalgia.

"Remi. Let me go inside."

His hand turned to a fist, but he kept it against the door. "You're my best friend," he breathed out with impatience and hurt. "How can you just throw out a decade of friendship?"

My mouth fell in shock. In utter surprise of his audacity.

Angrily, I spun around fast enough that I felt my hair whip in the wind. Remi breathed in harshly, and I hoped I smacked him with my hair.

When my glare found his, I shoved him back. He only stumbled a step before he straightened, but he thankfully didn't crowd me again.

"You're saying this to me? Me?" My voice raised a little higher in fury. "You did this! You cheated, so own up to it and deal with the consequences! Being drunk is not an excuse. If you were hurt, okay! You could have talked to me. You didn't have to cheat with Valerie!"

I could feel some eyes on us, but I was too busy fuming to care.

Remi's eyes turned black. "Right. I cheated with Valerie. She's just as guilty as me." He thrust his finger toward the door behind me and gritted through his teeth, "But she still gets to see you. She still lives with you. But I get kicked out?"

I threw my arms up in frustration. "She's on the lease! If it was up to me, I wouldn't see neither of you. So if you'll excuse me," I unlocked the door a little harder than necessary while keeping my eyes narrowed on him, "I want to leave. Get off my property, Remi."

He stayed rooted in his spot while I entered my house. I kept my eyes on him before breathing out harshly. "Also, tell your mom the truth. Or I will because we are not taking a break, Remi. We're done."

I slammed the door on his face the same moment his expression flamed with rage and defiance.

He didn't shout anything, nor did he bang on the door and demand my attention. Yet, I still found myself struggling to breathe while pressing my back against the cool surface. Once I managed to exhale without shaking, I closed my eyes and slid my bag off my shoulders.

Lazily, I kicked it toward the living room on my right. I let my gaze drift over the open space. The modern, olive green sofa was pressed against the wall on the right with two, vertical windows on either side. The view wasn't anything crazy since it faced the bungalow next to us.

There was a ivory carpet below the sofa, along with two round end tables. Each had a lamp, a candle and some books. The oval, walnut coffee table—which I insisted on buying because I needed to recline my body somehow—was empty and sat in the centre of the carpet. Next to the door I was leaning against was the TV, which hung soundly.

To my left was the glass, circular dining table that sat four people. Next to it was the kitchen that wasn't my favourite because of the dark mahogany kitchen cabinets. It also wasn't spacious because the peninsula was too close to the counter.

The door to Nellie's bedroom was the only one that sat at the front of the bungalow, right behind the kitchen table. While Valerie and Nellie shared a wall, Val's door was across from mine, on the right side of the kitchen. I was the only one that slept on the right side of the house, not that it mattered. There was maybe ten feet between mine and Valerie's doors. Fortunately, we had our own bathrooms. Another plus? She was close enough that I could hear when she leaves or arrives.

I avoid her like the plague.

My sigh was mixed exhaustion and sadness before I kicked off my shoes and headed toward the kitchen. There was only one way to cheer me up now, and that was a bowl of macaroni and cheese.

Knowing I had a little over an hour before Myles came over, I started taking out my ingredients—aka the-box, milk and butter—before jogging into my bedroom to take a shower. When I stepped back into the living area forty minutes later, I felt refreshed and smooth—the latter because I decided to shave my entire body. I hadn't originally planned on it, but when I saw the length of my leg hair, it reminded me that the last time I shaved was on Remi's birthday.

The thought made me bitter, but in the end I smiled because my legs were silky smooth again.

For the next thirty minutes, I shuffled around the apartment while waiting for the water to finish boiling the macaroni. When my timer went off, I moved to spill the water out.

I was about to pour the macaroni back into the pot when there was a sudden, hard knock on the front door.

My heart lurched in surprise before quickly realizing it must have been Myles. I turned off the stove before sprinting to the door. I managed to catch a breath before ripping the door open with a grin. "You're early."

His fluffy but well maintained eyebrow arched before his lips parted. I didn't let him say his sarcastic retort. Instead, I opened the door wider and ushered him in.

His eyes narrowed. I jerked my head inside before drawling, "I'm getting cold here, batman."

Despite agreeing to come over, he looked like he was entering his worst nightmare. Still, he took a wide step inside and moved his blank stare around the house. Once he was done assessing, he turned back to me.

"Up to your standards?" I teased, closing the door before circling him. "Or not what you were expecting?"

His gruff reply came a moment later. "Not as colourful as I expected it to be."

I grinned. "You really think I'm all princess-y, huh? I'm sorry to say that I don't like bright colours. They hurt my eyes." He cocked his head, and even though his expression remained empty, I could see him challenging my words. "Okay, I like pastel colours. But not neon colours. Some shades of yellow are nice, too. I like mustard. Not the sauce, the colour. Wait, is mustard even called a sauce? No, no it's a condiment. Like ketchup."

For the second time today, I didn't realize I'd been ranting until I finished. My face started twisting into a painful grimace while Myles looked like he was fighting back a smirk.

"Don't look at me like that," I grumbled before whirling toward the kitchen. I kept my back to him so he couldn't see my face flaming red.

Behind me, I could hear him taking off his shoes and jacket before plopping them somewhere. I poured the macaroni with its ingredients and started stirring when I felt him sitting on the bar stool in front of the peninsula.

"I brought you something," he deadpanned, sounding almost bored. Yet, when I spun around in surprise, I could see his jaw twitching anxiously.

At my wide eyes, he pressed his lips together before sliding a box of pencil crayons onto the counter, so it was directly in my line of sight. I tried to hide my gaping mouth but failed.

"W-why... you didn't have to bring me anything," I whispered in astonishment but still lifted the box to my chest. "Thank you."

He grunted and leaned back before crossing his bulky arms over his chest. "Not a big deal, princess. Heard somewhere you shouldn't go places empty handed."

I didn't want to mention that he could have brought anything, yet he chose to bring something that I actually appreciated. But I feel like if I mentioned him being kind, he'd deny it and leave without a second thought.

"Well, thanks anyway." My lips split into a wide grin. "I'll use them tonight. I needed new ones anyway. Some of my pencil crayons are shorter than my fingers."

His forehead creased in confusion before his focus fell to my fingers. They tightened around the box from his sudden attention.

"You colour that often?"

"Usually when I'm stressed." I smiled sheepishly before bringing the box to the counter. "It helps me calm down."

He considered my words with a thoughtful expression, so I used the moment of silence to continue stirring the macaroni. Once I saw everything blended, I turned off the stove before throwing Myles a look. "You sure you don't want?"

His nose flared. "What is it?"

"Mac and cheese." Not expecting that, his brows rose. "I don't really know how to cook, but mac and cheese has never failed me. I can make it home-made, but on nights like these, it's pre-made all the way."

"Nights like these?"

When I smiled this time, it felt forced. "Stressed," was all I said before turning back to my food. "So you want, batman? Or are you gonna watch me eat like a creeper?"

There was a long moment of silence before he said defensively, "I'm not a creeper." I hummed while taking two bowls from the upper cabinet on my right. "Fine. Whatever."

I smiled, thankful my back was still to him. "So, do you know how to cook?" I asked, mostly to make conversation but also because I was gen-uinely curious. Myles didn't seem like the type to make a whole gourmet meal, but he's taught me to stop judging people based on their looks.

Even though I trained my gaze to the food, the hairs on my neck rose when I felt his eyes on me. The temperature dropped a few degrees before he stated coolly, "I had to learn or I wouldn't be here."

Surprised by his statement, I turned around. At the same moment, Myles spun on the stool and avoided eye contact while lingering his gaze over the living room. I knew this was his own way of avoiding my impending question, so I let out a soft sigh before focusing on the mac and cheese again.

"You okay to eat in my room?" I asked lightly while using the wooden spoon to scoop the food into our bowls. "My roommates aren't here yet, but I don't know if you'd be okay if they saw you—"

"It's fine, princess." Even though his words came out sober, his voice wasn't hard anymore.

Bowls in hand, I twisted back to him and smiled. "Good." I shoved the bowl with more food toward him. "Take this. Do you want anything to drink?" He shook his head no, so I opened the drawer and grabbed two forks before rounding the peninsula. Once I stood in front of him, I grabbed the pencil crayons with my free hand while simultaneously jerking my chin to the far-right side of the house.

"That way, batman. Get up."

He smirked, amused with my commanding tone. Though, he didn't argue before striding toward my bedroom—which I cleaned, thank God. I didn't want to explain why I had days old clothes on my floor.

Myles stopped shortly once he entered my dark room. I side-stepped him and flicked on the light switch before setting the bowl and pencil crayons on the dresser across from my bed. I cursed when I remembered my laptop was still in my school bag.

"Gimme a second," I rushed out before jogging out of my bedroom. I reached the opposite side of the house and bent in front of my school bag. Once I had my laptop in hand, I slowed my pace but still walked fast until I was in my room again.

I nearly tripped on my feet when I took Myles in.

My bed was a queen and for my average height, it worked perfectly. But Myles—poor Myles—was almost a foot taller than me, and that was obvious now more than ever.

He sat on the left side of the bed, closest to the window, with his back pressed against the headboard. Even though a bed is my place of comfort, this man looked stiff as a rock, but that wasn't the only thing that caught my attention.

His feet were hanging off my bed.

I couldn't help but giggle. "You look ridiculous."

He glared but said nothing while I closed the door behind me. The motion had me tensing with the realization that I was about to be alone with Myles for the first time. Behind a closed door. With no wandering eyes around.

Hell, it was the first time I'd be alone with a guy who wasn't Remi. Yes, I had friends of the opposite sex, but they never found themselves in my bedroom.

It was too late to back-track. I finished closing the door, separating us from the rest of the house.

Myles watched me intently, but I didn't let him spot my sudden anxiety. Lowering my laptop onto the mattress, I made sure to grab my bowl from the dresser before sitting cross-legged next to him. I made sure there was a respectful distance between us before nestling the bowl in my lap.

"What we watching, princess?" He asked gruffly once I opened the streaming service.

Remembering my plan, I shoved all my anxious thoughts away and gave him a mischievous smile. "Well, batman," he rolled his eyes at his nickname, yet his lip twitched higher, "we are soft launching you into the world of Disney and Pixar."

His cocked his head, unamused. "And how will you be doing that?"

Swiftly, I pulled up one of my favourite cartoon films before whipping the screen in his direction. The moment his eyes landed on my laptop, I grinned and exclaimed, "We're watching Toy Story!"

"What the fuck is that?"

Finding his stupidity adorable, I wiggled in excitement. "The title kinda explains it. It's a toy's story. Their story as a toy."

He still looked disturbed, so I added amusingly, "These are toys that talk, but they have to hide from their owner that they can talk. In the first movie—"

"There's more than one?"

"There's five." If Myles was able to express normal emotions, I would have said he looked horrified. "Let's see how you like this one. We'll go from there."

He nodded begrudgingly, but when I grinned, his eyes fell to my lips and stayed there for less than a second before he lifted them back to mine. Some of harsh lines smoothed out from his face.

"Bowl ready?" I chirped and nodded once in satisfaction when he lifted it off my nightstand and sat it on his lap. "Good."

Dramatically, I pressed the play button before settling the laptop between our bodies. While the credits started rolling, I hesitantly glimpsed in his direction to see him already watching me.

"Listen, if you don't like it... can you tell me at the end of the movie? Don't knock it till you try it, right?"

He didn't say anything right away, but he didn't need to. He studied me with a hint of interest before twitching his head sideways. "You're telling me this movie is going to let me escape reality?" Shocked that he remembered why I liked watching these types of movies, I nodded dumbly.

He smirked humorlessly, like he thought otherwise. "Why do you wanna escape reality, princess? It not treating you well enough?"

I frowned and sat straighter. Vaguely, I heard the movie start but I was too engrossed by his question to care.

"That's not... that's not it." Taking a deep breath, I explained, "Reality sucks sometimes. Reality is actually a pain in the ass, but it's reality and we can't change it. But, we can escape it sometimes. Which everyone does in their own way." I flattened a palm on my chest and smiled. "I draw. I watch Disney. I star gaze. I—"

"Star gaze?"

I raised a brow and tsked. "You never experience disassociating until you look at the sky, Myles. I swear, I can do it for hours and won't even realize it."

"Anyway," I continued when he watched me silently, "We do things to step away from reality. You do it when you tattoo, don't you? Or when you watch Batman?"

Ignoring my teasing tone, he slightly narrowed his eyes. "But what are you escaping?"

"Are you forgetting my ex cheated on me with my roommate?" I tried to laugh, but it came out bitter. "You were there to witness it first hand, Myles."

"Are you still..."

When he didn't continue, I finished his sentence for him. "Sad? Hurt?" I shook my head softly. "Not really. Not anymore. It feels more like betrayal. And anger, at least when they try to defend themselves."

"Your boyfriend still defending himself?"

"Ex," I reminded him before snorting, "And yes. He was waiting in front of my house when I got home."

The energy around Myles felt tighter. Constricting. I noticed him clenching his jaw, and despite his stubble, I saw the muscle popping. "Did he do
anything to you?"

"Besides victim blaming himself? No." Frustrated, I scooped a spoonful
of mac and cheese and shoved it in my mouth. "Let's not talk about the
asshole."

His head cocked to the side and silently scrutinized me before questioning
a few seconds later, "So, which one is your favourite?" At my confused stare,
he nudged his head toward the laptop. "Movie."

Thankful he changed the topic, I smiled softly and admitted, "Tangled.
Eugene Fitzherbert can get it."

His face turned sour in disgust. "You like a character named Eugene?"

"You wouldn't understand." I sighed, making it seem like he was truly
missing out in the pleasure that was Flynn Rider. "You're totally making
conversation to avoid watching the movie, aren't you?"

He didn't answer my accusation, so I leaned forward and rewinded the
movie before gently smacking his shoulder. "Now. Watch."

□□□·□ □·□□□

I had to give it to him; despite all the huffing and puffing, Myles was
actually sitting still. More than that, he was actively watching the movie.

At one point, I got up to put our empty bowls on the dresser. But when
my eyes flickered to the new, unopened box of pencil crayons, I snatched
it up without another thought.

Myles kept quiet when I planted myself to his side again. I kept my attention on my laptop, realizing we were forty minutes in, while my hand
blindly reached for my nightstand. The moment my fingers grazed the

round knob, I pulled the first drawer open and pulled out my adult colouring book.

And by adult, it was pages of colourful words.

Not that I swore much out loud, but something about colouring "dirty" words—according to my parents—with bright colours always made me laugh.

Suddenly, I grinned with the realization that someone else might love this colouring book more than me.

"You wanna draw, batman?" I whispered and kept my smile buried when he whipped his head away from the screen. I didn't want to point out he was totally into in the movie, knowing he would deny it vigorously if I did. So I just lifted the colouring book and wiggled my eyebrows suggestively.

He stared at me blankly, so I mouthed, "You get to colour your favourite words."

A moment passed before he slowly lifted his hand out. I nearly whooped in excitement when I handed him the book. He barely skimmed the pages before he ripped out a random page and passed the book back to me. I hid my frown while he plucked out the black pencil crayon from the box.

So he would have a hard surface to draw on, I grabbed another colouring book from the nightstand and handed it to him. He was already using his leg as a surface, and it would have made me laugh, if it didn't work. Yet, he managed to draw without poking a hole through the paper.

"Here," I mumbled while sliding the book on his lap. I did my best to ignore the heat coming off him before turning to my own page. For the next ten minutes, we drew and watched Toy Story in silence, and I couldn't help but slowly relax—something that should scare me, considering I hardly ever relax because on most days, I felt like I was going on overdrive.

I was in the middle of using a pastel pink to draw flowers over the large F when Myles slid his paper over my work.

My mouth opened to teasingly scold him for ruining my work—until I really looked at his drawing.

It was a drawing. Instead of using the page for its intended purpose, he had flipped it over and used the blank white canvas to do something on his own. And he drew Woody.

My jaw dropped before I could stop myself. "You did this?" I asked dumbly, not even trying to lower my voice.

If he responded, I didn't hear him. I was completely captivated by his work because in the span of ten minutes, he sketched a character he's barely familiar with. And he did it with detail. Although, I couldn't help but realize he didn't colour it in, despite the endless amount of crayons splayed out between us.

"No wonder you got into tattooing," I mumbled before flashing him a small smile. "Are you gonna colour it in?"

"No."

My forehead creased. "You said that way too fast."

"Because I don't colour."

"Oh, I'm sorry. I forgot you're too broody to use colour." Despite my joking tone, he kept his expression blank. I rolled my eyes and searched for the beige pencil crayon—which is hard to do, considering the only source of light in the room is from the laptop. "Fine. I'll do it."

I let out a breath when I found it a few seconds later, halfway sticking out from underneath his thigh. I grinned in satisfaction before starting the base layer.

Once finished, I leaned back and considered what I should do next until I felt goosebumps trickling my arms. I slowly stiffened before peering to Myles, only to see his eyes on me.

Feeling my throat constricting, I tried to lighten the air by teasing, "What? You want to colour now?"

He shook his head once, never pulling his eyes off mine. "Go ahead, princess."

With that short encouragement. I smiled and continued drawing his sketch. And I continued doing so, even after the first movie finished. Even after he lazily deadpanned I could play the second movie.

I tried not to smile brightly before doing as he instructed.

I wasn't sure when I fell asleep.

All I knew was that my neck had a crick from being tucked in a unnatural degree. It wasn't until I felt a finger twitching on my waist did I realize that I was sleeping on my side—and I wasn't alone.

The hand was large enough to wrap the entire curve of my waist. And it was warm—not sweaty warm, but a soothing warmth.

Myles and I were sleeping. On the same bed. And he was touching me.

Why wasn't I pulling away again?

Oh yeah. Warmth. It was nice.

But this was Myles, I remembered in a panic. Myles who I was almost friends with. Someone who sometimes scared the bejeezus out of me.

The moment I came to that realization, I started to squirm away.

My shuffling came to a screeching halt, however, when I heard loud thumps coming from outside my bedroom door.

It wasn't a second later until my bedroom door was violently thrown open, and then everything happened so fast.

The hand on my waist vanished. The mattress aggressively bounced as Myles moved, followed by a piercing scream.

In the next second, I scrambled up and widened my eyes to see Nellie by the front door with a horrified expression. All while Myles sat on the bed with a gun pointed at her.

□□□·□ □·□□□

whoop whoop cliffhanger

finally the weekend has arrived, and I can write :)

I've finally found the inspiration to write again, so I'm excited to soon announce that my new book is coming to you next spring !

Hope you loves have a great Friday x

Chapter 7

C HAPTER VIIAsking For Help

I watched the scene in front of me with dread. It wasn't until Nellie screamed I was able to slowly come back to reality.

"What the fuck!" She screeched in fury but didn't move a muscle, probably frightened he would shoot if she moved.

Shakily, I twisted my head to see Myles looking at Nellie stonily. Almost if he was having an out of body experience.

"That's Nellie. You... you met her at the bar, remember?"

He didn't make an effort to move, so I hesitantly brought my hand on his wrist and sighed in relief when I felt his muscles relaxing. When he jerked the gun to his lap and turned on the safety, I dumbly whispered, "You have a gun?"

More rigid than ever, he yanked my touch off him before throwing himself off the bed. My mouth fell in surprise when he grabbed his belongings and stomped toward the exit—which Nellie jumped away from.

The house was eerily silent until the door slammed closed seconds later, making us both flinch.

I pinched my eyes shut, just as Nellie hissed, "What the hell was that about, Allie?"

□□□·□ □·□□□

The library was so quiet that as I shuffled my way to the exit, anyone could hear the faintest creek of the panelled floors. Every sound made me cringe, knowing that it would bring unwanted attention.

Granted, I was one of the last few people in the library, with it being eleven at night. The library closes at midnight, and most people left hours ago. Unfortunately for me, I had articles to submit for the school's newspaper, and a term paper to write.

Ever since finishing class at six, I'd been working. While I am happy I got most of my work done, I was ravenous. But that could be because I decided to starve myself until I finished. It would be like a reward.

The thought of class reminded me of Nellie's cold shoulder. We both took a news reporting class from twelve-to-three, and normally our walk to campus never had a quiet moment. But after what happened with Myles Tuesday night, she's been avoiding me. After admitting that I didn't know he had a gun, Nellie went from frightened to disappointed mom mode.

"You've talked to this guy for a month, Althea. How could you not know he owns a gun. Hell, he not only owns it, he carries it on him! He brought it to our house!"

She was upset, and she had every right to be.

And... I was upset, too. If I had to admit it, I had been scared for a fleeting minute. Scared of him or for him, I didn't know.

I haven't spoken to him since then, nor has he tried to contact me and try to explain his reasoning. One for carrying a gun, and two, that his first instinct was to pull it out when he heard a noise.

This experience should finalize how much Myles is not my type. We're complete opposites. Not only in personality, but now that he has a gun, while I hate the idea of them.

Remembering why I hate them made my thoughts darken, but thankfully, my stomach growled and reminded me that I was hungry.

The moment I strode outside, I shivered when a blast of cold wind crushed into me. I hastily zipped my thin jacket all the way to my neck and stuffed my hands into my pockets before waddling across the street. Even though I welcomed the chill most days, I hated how much that changed when my ears weren't covered. Even with long hair, it failed to protect me from the frigid air.

Spotting a sandwich shop a few stores away from me, I quickened my pace—until I heard a familiar, gruff voice bite out my name. "Althea!"

I came to an abrupt pause when I heard feet pounding against the sidewalk from behind. Not a moment later, Myles came to a stop in front of me, heaving angrily while his small, darkened eyes wandered over me. I couldn't help but do the same to him.

Myles appeared the exact same since I last saw him—which wasn't surprising and yet, I didn't know what I expected. For him to grow a whole freaking beard in the two days we haven't talked?

Something close to fear had me nervously treading backward when I realized the last time I saw him, it was with a gun pointing at my friend's chest. I know he didn't do it intentionally, but I couldn't help but feel anxious around someone who's first instinct is to pull out a gun the moment they're faced with something—or someone—unfamiliar to them.

His eyes flashed with anger when he saw me rocking back. "Are you scared of me?"

Despite looking angry, he sounded almost... disappointment.

"No," I choked out before clearing my throat. I wrapped my arms around me when a strong gust of wind blew toward me. "I'm just a jumpy person. I jump around."

He stared at me plainly, recognizing my obvious lie. But instead of calling me out, he clenched his jaw before shoving a hand into his jacket pocket. I watched with furrowed brows as he took out a grey... is that a toque hat?

My jaw dropped, and before I realized what was happening, Myles' arms stretched out. He didn't ask my permission before tugging the hat onto my head. I felt his fingers hover close to my ear, almost as if he was making sure they were covered before he pulled himself back.

Absently, I touched my head. "Why—"

"I have a hat, you don't," he stated harshly. "I can see your ears getting red from here. You can give it back to me later."

I nodded but couldn't help but eye him suspiciously.

"You weren't home."

For a moment, I blinked. Then blinked again. Weren't. How would he know that unless—

"Did you go to my house?" I demanded.

Despite witnessing my apparent anger, Myles' face remained blank. "You ignored my last two messages. We need to talk."

"Messages? I didn't get any messages." He arched a brow, almost challeng- ingly. With an huff, I slid my bag off my shoulders. I held onto the handle and aimlessly reached inside until I felt my fingers grazing the phone. I pulled it out and... yeah, he texted me thirty minutes ago.

"I wasn't ignoring you," I admitted sheepishly while sliding my arms through the straps. I lifted my eyes to his and saw him already watching me. "I was at the library, so my phone was off."

My eyes lingered over his expression before asking slowly, "What did you want to talk about?"

With a slight cock of his head, he studied me. "You don't like guns." He said this matter-of-factly.

"No, I love them. I dance around them in my free time, praising the God's for the wondrous gift that is guns. I just love weapons of mass destruction." He didn't find my sarcasm funny, so I dropped my tight smile and sighed. "Myles, I... I grew up Detroit. And I grew up watching the news. Hearing them list all the gun violence in the city? I witnessed someone getting shot in front of me, Myles. In a convenience store. He looked like he was my age."

"You know how people say sometimes time goes by in slow motion when you're in front of danger? They're right. I've never been so scared for my life that day. He survived, and still, all I remember is the gun going off. The body falling to the ground. Blood... blood everywhere. So, yeah. I really, really don't like guns."

I hadn't realized his face softened until I gasped for air I desperately needed. "I keep a gun on me because I grew up in a shitty area. The second I was old enough, I got a license. So I'd never be unprotected again. I'm not sorry for having a gun, princess. But I am sorry that I scared you enough to make you stop asking your millions of questions."

Kicking non-existent rocks under my feet, I lowered my head and mumbled, "I don't ask a million questions."

He responded with silence, but I knew he was smirking.

"Not million, princess. Millions."

Shooting my gaze to his, I narrowed my eyes. "You're mean."

"Never denied that."

I rolled my eyes and fought a smile before recalling what he'd said. That was enough to make me purse my lips together. "Are you okay?" I asked softly before reiterating, "I mean, you said you never wanted to be unprotected again. Did you get hurt?"

He gave me tense smile. "Nothing for you to think about, princess. It's in the past."

"Just because something is in the past doesn't mean it's not important," I pointed out before asking again, "Seriously, Myles. Do you want to talk about it?"

This time he didn't smile. "I'll walk you home."

"You don't have to—" He strode past me, in the direction of my place.

Not wanting to challenge his stubbornness, I sighed and spun around before breaking into a light jog. I caught up to him a second later. "Did you go to my house because you missed me?" I chirped, deciding to lighten the mood.

Myles' nose scrunched in disgust, like the thought of him displaying any positive feeling was enough to induce vomit.

"Where would you get that ridiculous idea?"

"It's called reading between the lines," I joked before moving my head forward. I felt his gaze burning on the side of my face. "You texted me, and when I didn't reply, you came over."

"Because I don't like being ignored."

"Ah, yes. Because you like to do the ignoring."

He didn't confirm nor deny that.

"It's okay, I won't tell anyone if you're worried you'll lose your street cred."

He snorted in disbelief. "Street cred?"

"I don't know... don't tattoo artists want to appear all cool and stuff? Granted, I've never met one besides you, but I think you'd be a horrible example on how tattoo artists act. You don't even colour in the things you make! You are an anomaly. Wait, is that the right word? I think it is. You're unique. There. You know what, if I get a tattoo, I'll go to someone and get back to you on that whole attitude thing. I know they say three is a pattern, but I think two is one too, right? God, I should not be a scientist or whoever does labs. Validity and reliability? What's that? I don't know."

Realizing that I'd been talking non-stop for over a minute, my face contorted as if I was in physical pain. I had to stop myself from slapping myself in the face. "I told you to shut me up when I ramble," I cried out.

"Five dollars in the question jar," he hummed in amusement.

"We're not actually doing that!"

For the next few minutes, we went back and forth on the pros and cons on having a question jar. While he had at least five benefits, I had zero. So, when I offered a cuss jar for him, that's when he went silent.

"Uh-huh. That's what I thought," I said smugly.

"You're goddamn fucking mouth," he grumbled roughly.

I grinned. "I already have fifteen dollars."

His feet were pounding a little harder on the sidewalk. I tried to stifle my chuckle at the obvious sign of his displeasure, but I must have failed because a second later, he was glaring at me. I didn't cower. Instead, my eyes drifted toward the hair he had pulled back in a low bun.

"Don't your ears get cold too?" I started to reach for the hat I'm wearing. "You should take this ba—"

"If I wanted to wear the hat, I would have worn the hat. Keep it."

At that moment, we reached the end of the strip. When we turned right, my eyes dropped to the driveway coming in view, and I couldn't help but remember Friday, when he came by and walked to the club with me. Then my thoughts wandered to the realization I had later that night...

My steps faltered, and I nearly fell on the pavement until a strong arm wrapped itself around my waist, hoisting me back on my feet. "Jesus fucking Christ, princess. If you keep this up, you're gonna fall."

"If I fall on grass I'll be fine." I grinned as he let me go with a shake of his head. "I was just thinking that maybe you should help me with my list. Become a more active member, if you get what I'm saying."

Maybe my lack of filter was a good thing, because I got to witness the utter horror painted on Myles' expression. He almost tripped before he unfortunately caught himself. I would have felt embarrassed for my brassiness, if I wasn't struggling to hold back my laughter.

Slowly, he stopped walking and twisted his body, so he was completely facing me.

"I'm already helping you," he stated gruffly, almost slowly, as if he was trying to play dumb.

I nodded quickly. "Yes, but now I want you to fuck me."

Again, he looked so horrified that I didn't feel the need to hit myself in self-disgust. I struggled to stop myself from grinning because I never thought my bluntness would be useful, let alone not humiliating. But here I am, making Myles—only-has-five-emotions Myles—use every bit of his facial muscles.

He shook his head, hastily wiping away his expression. "You're sleep deprived. Go sleep."

"It's a good idea—"

He laughed darkly and lowered his chin, so shadows eclipsed his features. "It is not a good idea, princess."

I crossed my arms and raised my brows, only to feel them brush against the hat. "Well, I disagree. I've been thinking about this since Friday," his head shot back in surprise, but I continued, "and normally friends-with-benefits never work out. But we don't have history that would stop us. We've known each other for a month! You're always talking about being safe, not going to a sex club, blah, blah, blah—"

He glared. "You still want to go to a fucking sex club? I told you—"

"Yes, I know! It's dangerous. But I know you. At least well enough that I can trust you with this. Tell me why it wouldn't be a good idea."

He rubbed his face with evident frustration. "Jesus fucking Christ." Once he lowered his hand, he gave me a dead stare. "You aren't a casual type of woman, princess. You need romance. Seriousness. For fucks sake, you watch Disney movies for fun. I can't give you that."

"I'm asking you to fuck me, batman. Not go on one knee and propose." I frowned. "What, do you think I'll magically fall in love with you? You aren't really my type."

"But I'm your type to fuck?" He smirked before quickly sobering. "I don't do fluff."

"Then don't do it." I smiled and shrugged faintly. "And do you want me to call you pretty, Myles? You are very pretty."

My confession seemed to silence him. His mouth opened and closed for a few seconds while his eyes lingered over me. I couldn't help but wonder if he's ever been complimented.

"You're clearly not seeing why this isn't a good deal," he gritted.

I frowned. "It's not a big deal."

He laughed humorlessly before taking a step forward. I inhaled sharply when he got rid of most of the space between us—enough that I caught a whiff of a scent that seemed to follow him; cedarwood.

"Not a big deal?" His voice lowered dangerously while keeping eye contact with me. "I have a very low self-control, princess. Do you really wanna poke this bear?"

My mouth opened, but no sound came out. His gaze lowered and watched while I slowly swallowed, trying to figure out what to say. He actually managed to silence me.

Suddenly wanting to defend him, I unfastened my mouth to speak, but I was quickly cut off by the sound of laughter coming somewhere behind me. Myles was first to shoot his gaze off mine, and when I saw him glare, I frowned and followed where his attention laid.

A group of three guys seemed to round the corner onto the street, but instead of walking any further, they remained next to the crosswalk. The streetlights let me see how their heads turned in our direction, but one guy with blonde hair wore a smirk. When our eyes met, it widened before he turned to his friends and laughed at whatever they said.

Behind me, I felt Myles stiffening.

"What's so fucking funny, donkey?"

I choked on saliva.

Did Myles just call one of them a donkey?

I think I was so shocked that I didn't realize Myles stepped around me until his back was blocking my sight. Still, I could hear some of them snickering. I swiftly moved to stand next to Myles, the same moment two brunettes stumbled next to their blond friend. I realized then that they were probably drunk.

"Myles, let's go," I mumbled under my breath. When he didn't even try to move, I wrapped my fingers around his bicep and gently tugged him back. His feet remained in place.

The blond guy took a uneven step forward. I noticed that they never stopped looking at each other. Am I third wheeling, or is someone going to throw a fist?

"You speak English? ¿O tengo que hablarte como un idiota?"

My eyes rounded. Myles spoke Spanish?

Even though he never turned his face to me, I studied the side of his expression. The tan skin and angular features that made every part of his face defined and sharp. I glanced at his thick, nearly black hair and wondered what it would look like outside of the confines of the bun. I knew his eyes were small and downturned despite them being off me. Even though this answered one of my thousands of questions about Myles, another million questions sprouted.

Wait... did I not even know his last name?

I was ready to slap myself in the face, but that screeched to a halt when I heard Myles gritting next to me, "What the fuck did you just say?"

I pushed my head back in surprise by his lethal tone. He sounded like he was struggling to contain his temper.

The blond man must have not noticed this as he laughed in disbelief. "Bro, the pussy can't be that good. Relax."

He barely finished his sentence before Myles strode forward. By the time I opened my mouth to stop him, he already reached the three guys and either punched their face or kicked the back of their legs. I watched, jaw on the floor, as the drunk men collapsed before trying to get up.

Myles snarled when one of them tried to grab his leg and bring him down. They barely moved him an inch before Myles kicked them in the face.

I internally gagged when I saw blood coming out of his nose. Thankfully, I managed to unlatch myself from my spot before running toward him.

"Myles!" I hissed and grabbed his hand this time, with my nails digging into his flesh to snap him out of whatever came over him. "Enough. We're going."

He didn't budge, so I turned back to him and glared. "Either we leave now, or the next hit you throw, I'll move in front." I was bluffing, but Myles didn't call me out.

Even though his eyes still flared with blood thirst, he followed me the short distance back home. Once I was sure he wouldn't run back to the guys, I let go of his hand and unlocked the door with a clenched jaw.

Opening the door wider, I flicked on the lights and let Myles welcome himself in while I took off my shoes and stomped to the kitchen. Valerie's car wasn't in the driveway, and Nellie would be working late for her internship, so I knew we had the place to ourselves, free to talk however loud we wanted.

Yet, I remained silent and rummaged through the kitchen cupboards while simultaneously ignoring Myles loud footfalls.

I exhaled when I opened the bottom right cupboard and found what I was looking for.

Once I stood upright, I spun on my heel but stopped short when I saw Myles watching me by the edge of the peninsula. Now able to see him under good lighting, I noticed some strands beginning to crowd the front of his face. His eyes still seemed wild, but when they fell on me, he stretched out his chest as he breathed in sharply.

When I said nothing, his jaw bobbed in frustration. "Still wanna sleep with me, princess?"

My mouth unfurled. "Is that why you did that?" I almost screeched before slamming the first aid kit on the counter. "Are you trying to prove a freaking point?!"

"I'm not proving a point. This is who I am," he grounded through his teeth angrily. "You just like seeing everything in fucking rainbows and butterflies."

"That is not true!"

He laughed harshly. "You trust me, princess. That's the stupidest thing you could ever do."

"Why? Because you like to paint yourself as a bad guy?" I gestured to him in anger before throwing my arms up. "You're doing such a great job. Do want a freaking academy award?"

"What's wrong with me trusting you with this? You've given me no reason not to to trust you. Until right now." I grumbled the last part to myself as I lowered my head to the ground, but I heard Myles roughly sucking his breath.

Neither of us spoke, so I moved around the peninsula and sidestepped him before dragging the first aid kit on the counter, in front of the bar stool. Myles followed my silent instructions and sat down while I went back inside the kitchen to grab a kitchen towel and our cheap vodka.

When I stopped in front of him again, I heatedly snapped the lid off before pouring a decent amount onto the cloth. I will admit to grabbing Myles hand a little to roughly before dropping the cloth on his cut knuckles.

His snarled, "Fuck."

Fuck you, I wanted to say, but I didn't have the strength to. Because despite him trying to portray himself as a villain, I hated that it wouldn't work. I hated that I couldn't hate him because I knew that despite his short temper, he was good. He helped me when I was a stranger. The least I could do was help him as a friend. Even if he was a total asshole.

I felt his eyes on me the entire time I was cleaning his hands. At one point, I saw his chin lowering, as if he was trying to catch my eyes, but I adamantly avoided him. I feared that if he gave me a single look, I'd lose my composure.

Once I finished wrapping the gauze around his knuckles—again a little tighter than necessary—in the corner of my eye, I saw him slowly sagging.

"I'm sorry," he grumbled, almost reluctantly. My hands froze as I was about to secure the gauze. I kept my eyes narrowed on his hands before slowly continuing what I was doing.

He exhaled loudly. "Stop that."

"Stop what?"

When he didn't reply, I forced my head up and met his waiting gaze. His eyes blazed when he saw my blank expression. "Stop looking at me like that."

"Like what?"

His palpable frustration almost made me smile. My questions annoyed him, and yet, he didn't call me out as he explained, "Like you don't like me."

For some reason, that broke my heart and made me smile at the same time. "Do you want me to like you?"

Myles' face contorted in disgust as his nose flared. "Not like that."

I couldn't help but laugh. "Damn, tell me how you really feel."

For the first time since he sat down, I saw his muscles relaxing. Once the gauze was secured, I moved back and packed everything back into the plastic, blue briefcase.

He didn't immediately jump off the stool, so after a few seconds, I gingerly asked, "Why did you start that fight?"

I turned my head to see a dark shadow clouding his expression. "I'm an asshole. That's who I am." He paused and quickly snapped his eyes over my face before he clenched his jaw and looked away. "Plus, they shouldn't talk to you like that. They had it coming."

For a moment, all I did was watch him with conflicting emotions. In the years I've known Remi, and the two years we dated, he never defended me. That could be because he believed I could stand up for myself, but it was also because he was the least confrontation person I've ever met. I never knew what it felt like to be defended—but was he right? I didn't like the idea of Myles getting himself hurt because of me, but at the same time, he cared enough to defend me.

Teasingly, I said, "It sounds like you like me, batman."

He glared at his feet and pursed his lip, almost as if he was bitter about that fact. "You're tolerable."

"Tolerable?" I gasped mockingly. "I'm hurt."

"It's your questions, princess. And your never-ending optimism. It's disgusting."

I rocked back and laughed. "Disgusting? You're such a grump."

He looked at me and said nothing before his focus flickered to my head. I touched the top, only to realize I was still wearing his hat.

"Here," I said, handing it to him. "Thanks for that. I'm sorry if you got cold without it."

"I told you, princess. Cold doesn't affect me."

"Why not?" I finally got to ask. "Did you grow up somewhere in Canada? Like way up North?"

Just like that, his expression completely closed off, ridding me from seeing any emotion from him. I started to frown and demand why the change in mood when he shot up from the stool and took long strides to the entrance.

Without turning to me, he called out, "Thanks for the hand, princess. Gotta go."

"Myles," I called out, but he never stopped moving. Not when he got his feet into his shoes, and not when he went through the door.

Still keeping his back to me, he coolly said, "Don't open the door for strangers," before closing the door behind him.

I had to pick my jaw off the floor. Was this dude being serious?

Scrunching my nose, I dramatically mimicked, "Don't open the door for stranger," while tossing the garbage out. He pretended like he didn't just act like a stranger.

□□□·□ □·□□□

happy Friday loves! Tomorrow is my writing day so I'm EXTRA happy ;)

I hope everyone is enjoying the story so far, I hope you like Myles and Althea as much as I do <3

Chapter 8

C HAPTER VIIIThe Rules

□□□·□ □·□□□

Mac and cheese sang the words to my soul. The taste. The smell. The feeling of the fork gliding through the milky cheese before you squeezed slightly hard and plucked the macaroni out from the bowl...

Moisture built up in my mouth before I hastily resumed the making of my favourite, grown-up meal. Grown up was used very, very lightly.

Sometimes, it was scary. I was twenty-one—my birthday was on June 29 so I am still young—but most days, I felt like I was a teenager in an adults body. Especially when I was reminded that I was graduating from my undergrad in a few months. For heaven's sake, I still remember my high school graduation. Vividly. But now I have to be an adult? I don't even know how to do my taxes properly! Or how to have a mortgage!

But one thing that will never fail me is food. I love food. And cheese. Damn, I love cheese. Mac and cheese.

I smiled to myself before focusing on the task at hand; making my home-made mac and cheese. I finally was able to sit down—metaphorically—and make my own meal, instead of relying on boxed food. My last midterm had been yesterday, so for the time being, I'm free.

Excitingly enough, March began. I didn't necessarily hate winter, but I loved when the weather started to warm up. I loved the in-between be-tween seasons. And right now, we were getting a taste of some warmth.

Peering inside the pot, I grinned when I saw the cheese perfectly melted. I quickly turned off the stove and slid the pot to the back burner before opening the upper cabinet and pulling out a bowl. In that same moment, my ears perched at the sound of a door opening.

When I realized it was coming from my right—in the direction of the narrow hallway—I stiffened. While my room was there, so was...

I heard soft feet pausing at the entrance to the open concept living room/kitchen/dining room combo.

With my shoulders pressed back, I slowly manoeuvred myself closer to the counter while keeping my back toward the newcomer. The silence allowed me to catch her breathing in sharply before she rounded the peninsula. In this moment, I cursed the rental gods for giving us a small kitchen.

I did my best to scoop as much food in my bowl as possible while I felt her moving around behind me. When I began to hover the lid over the pot, I heard a pair of feet making a scratching noise against the floorboard. I knew it was because of the house shoes she wore daily.

"Are you just going to ignore me? Not even say hi?" An irate voice said.

Forcing calm, positive thoughts in my head, I tightly smiled. "Hi, Valerie."

"Wow, that's so much better," she bit out before stopping next to me. I tried my best not to grit my teeth before tilting my head in her direction. In that moment, breathing felt harder.

Valerie wore a matching gym set that included an intricate sports bra and leggings with side pockets. It was a light sage green colour that complimented her clear, porcelain skin. When I turned my attention to her face, I couldn't help but notice the mixture of pain and frustration she wore—she typically did her best not to scrunch up her face too much, and yet, her brows were furrowed.

My gaze fell to her hair in realization that she dyed it again. It grew out to above her breasts, and instead of blonde highlights, she mixed it with a lighter brown.

"Thea," she said in exasperation. I flickered my gaze to her slightly hooded, emerald green eyes. "Can we please talk? I know you're still mad, but I never meant to hurt you—"

"Maybe you didn't mean to, but you did." Twisting my body so I was facing her, I rested my hip to the counter. "There's no way this can be fixed, Valerie."

I sounded so resigned. I'm not sure when, but I think I abandoned my anger about the situation. There wasn't anything I could do, so why would I dwell over it? Even though there was a sting of betrayal every time I recalled seeing them together on the couch, I've started to let it go. But at the same time, things wouldn't be as it used to. I'm still surprised Valerie and Remi thought they could worm themselves out from the situation they made. Was I really that big of a pushover that they thought I'd welcome them back with open arms?

She huffed, her expression twisting in irritation. "It's been over a month. We live together, you can't honestly keep this up."

"You chose to stay, Val."

Hearing my calm tone, she glared. "So, that's it? This is done?"

"I don't know what you want me to say. You slept with my boyfriend." When she opened her mouth, I raised my hand to stop her. "Yeah, I know you guys were drunk. I get it. But... you can't do things and expect there to be no consequence."

"What, so I'm being punished?" Her eyes flared. "Maybe he took advantage of me!"

I gave her a bored look. "Valerie. I saw you guys. You were literally on top of him." She cringed at the memory. "And you said it yourself; you were both drunk. You guys took advantage of each other."

"If you want to be civil, I can be civil." To try to prove my point, I smiled, albeit, tensely. "But we're not friends. After school finishes, we'll probably never see each other again."

For a split second, I saw her eyes shining with unshed tears before she swiftly lowered her gaze to the floor. I hated how much it affected me, despite all that she's done. I hated that I felt bad for hurting her feelings.

There was a short pause before she met my eyes again. But this time, any sadness was gone and replaced with resentment.

"You don't want to be friends? Fine. We won't be friends," she spat before stomping out of the kitchen. I watched in disbelief as she strode to her bedroom before slamming the door behind her.

Slowly, I glanced at the bowl of mac and cheese in my hands. I regretted being in the kitchen now.

□□□·□ □·□□□

Meet me at the bar.

Was I at the right bar? I mean, there were six bars on this street alone. But at the same time, where else would he expect us to meet? This was the bar. Where we met. So he'd show up. Right?

Overthinking was my friend at the moment, so I decided to raise my hand and get the bartenders attention. He was making a drink in front of me, so I quickly asked, "Can I have a double shot of vodka? Your cheapest." I'm used to drinking cheap alcohol. Living near campus forced you to have low standards if you wanted to remain... well, not poor.

He tightly smiled in acknowledgement, and after a few seconds, he handed me a shot. When I told him to open a tab for me, I took the shot with a slight grimace.

I wasn't sure what I expected when I got Myles' text over an hour ago. I haven't heard from him in the last few days, and because I'd been busy with school and the newsletter, I hadn't reached out. So, I was thoroughly surprised when he texted me right after I finished class at six.

Granted, I could have totally come to the bar right after class—it was on my way home, anyways. But in the end, I found myself rushing home and slipping into a short black dress before fixing my wavy hair into a sleek back ponytail.

I shamelessly also shaved my armpits and... some other places. In my defence, when winter came, so did my body hair.

But I am horny. I admit it! I am a twenty-one-year-old that has never had good sex. And since making my list, I've wanted to have sex. I am deprived. I want to check off my freaking list. I'm itching for it.

So, if Myles decides he doesn't want this—totally understandable—I'm leaving the bar with a guy.

But sitting inside the bar now, I think my options were quite slim.

While I didn't keep up with hockey, I knew there was a game today because Nellie said she wanted to go with some friends. I also heard Valerie on the phone earlier today. She also mentioned heading out, so I knew I'd have the house to myself.

But I realized, this game was a blessing and a curse because the bar had no hot guys. There were a few groups of guys, yes, but they all looked like they just got out of high school and probably had fake IDs. Were they legal? Totally. But unlike John Mayer, I don't date nineteen-year-old's.

I was fidgeting in my seat when I asked for another double shot. The moment it was delivered, I threw my head back and drank it in one gulp. By the time I brought the glass back to the counter, I felt a cool chill run down my bare back as the front door opened behind me.

Spinning the stool around, my lips instantly pulled into a grin when I saw Myles striding inside the bar, only to come to a sharp halt when he saw me sitting across from him. It felt like my heart was in my throat when his eyes travelled down my body. I did the same to him.

I could tell he just got off from work, but that didn't stop him from not looking good. Even though his hair was still pulled back in a bun, he wore black jeans and a black shirt underneath his open puffer jacket.

He dropped his head and clenched his jaw before removing the distance between us.

"Why do you look like that?"

I couldn't help but grin wider at his demanding tone. "Well, if I'm going to ask for help to complete my sex list, I might as well look the part."

A few heads shot in my direction, but I didn't feel embarrassed. The alcohol was already worming itself into my system. Thank god for being a light weight.

He bared his teeth before giving a vicious glare at the people staring at me. When he turned back to me, I saw his face red with anger.

Without pulling his eyes off mine, he stuffed a hand into his jean pocket and removed his wallet. With one hand, he pulled out a fifty and gave it to the bartender while grabbing my elbow with the other.

I almost fell off the chair, but he quickly caught me before snatching my jacket off the stool. I yelped when he tugged me out of the bar, not really focusing on where he was taking me until my back was pressed against a cool surface.

I quickly realized that he snuck us into the alley beside the bar. Surprised by the lack of light shining at us, I glanced to the left with a frown, only to see a large dumpster truck hiding us from people's view.

The sound of low grumbling made me twist my head back to Myles, only to see him opening my jacket for me to wear. I grinned and slipped my arms inside while asking gleefully, "So, did you think about it? No pressure, obviously, but I'm just letting you know that I've decided to get dicked down tonight. Do you know when you feel so overwhelmingly stressed that you can't do anything but feel anxiety? And then when all that stress is gone, you feel empty? So you look for what can replace that empty feeling, only to realize, you feel empty because your pussy is empty!" I heaved in laughter at my own joke while Myles looked horrified. "Anyway, I finished all my tests and upcoming assignments, so I feel empty. I want sex. Listen, you don't wanna help a friend out, that's cool but don't stop me from getting—"

"If you say dicked down again, I'm going to fucking hurl, princess."

I grinned toothily. "Now I don't need to. Can you say that again?" He bared his teeth and grumbled some more, all while stuffing his hand into his jacket pocket. "If you're really worried, we can make rules."

He said nothing before he plopped something on my head. I frowned and touched my scalp, only to realize he put a hat on me. When did he have a hat? Am I going crazy? Was he always wearing a hat?

Noticing my expression, he flared his nose. "You're fucking shaking like a leaf."

"That could be because I'm wearing a dress," I offered jokingly, but clearly by his tight features, he didn't find it funny. "What crawled up your ass, batman? I told you before I'm used to dressing like this in the winter. Save money on the commute when you can just walk places."

"Doesn't matter. You can get sick."

I rolled my eyes playfully. "Says the guy that says the cold doesn't bother him. Maybe you can get sick." He watched me soberly before his head tilted toward the alleyway exit. "What are you thinking about?"

He silently exhaled. "Thinking about dragging you back inside."

"How about you drag me to my place?" I teased before laying my hand on his shoulder. He stiffened beneath my touch, and despite wearing a puffy jacket, I felt the heat coming from his thick muscles.

He's so freaking big, my thoughts intrusively said, almost in awe. I shoved it away because if we were going to do this, we'd do this with no feelings.

"Didn't you say if I flirt, that means I want it?" I drawled, making his eyes flash as he remembered what he told me two weeks ago. "Well, I want it."

"And I've really thought about it too," I rushed out before lifting my hands. "We'd have rules. Like no kissing. You know, because that makes things emotional and stuff."

Myles couldn't stop his lip from lifting in a small smirk. "And stuff?"

"Yeah. Plus, maybe you slobber like a dog. Wouldn't want that. My friend told me about this guy she kissed. Said it was like kissing a frog. But not the good kind. Wait, I'm not saying there's a good frog to kiss, but you know the whole, kiss a frog and he'll turn into a prince? Well this dude was not turning into a prince. If anything, he made princes sound disgusting to be around." I paused, thinking again about my favourite Disney movies. "I think I'm being a hypocrite because I actually liked Princess and The Frog. Oh, but I said dog, not frog. So I'm not a hypocrite." I breathed in relief before blinking back to Myles. "What was I saying again?"

His lips were pulled into a tight line, as if he was holding himself back from smiling. "Kissing," he drawled in a low rumble.

"Ah," I dragged out with a nod. "Yeah, so no kissing. And also no sleep-overs. It'll make sex more impersonal."

His eyes slowly dragged over me, but I didn't know if he was assessing me or the situation. After a few moments, he shook his head once.

"I wish I could say you're only saying this because you're drunk, but I know you'd say this sober." He gave me a small, crooked smile. "The only thing that's different is that you're not telling me you want to hit yourself."

"Slap," I corrected, which only made him sigh. "Anyway, I'm not drunk. I'm a little tipsy, but that can be easily solved. By fucking me."

Instead of giving me a response I wanted, he exploded. With laughter, I mean.

I pursed my lips while he struggled to contain himself. I was flattered that I made him laugh again, but also offended.

"Is my flirting not good enough for you?"

This time, he didn't stop his amused grin. "No, princess. You did amazing." With a disbelieved short laugh, he reminded me, "And sorry to break it to you, princess, but we already broke your second rule."

I frowned in confusion, filing through my memories, but I came out short. "When did we have a sleepover?"

He sobered, waiting a few long seconds before deadpanning, "When you forced Disney on me."

"I did not force Disney on you," I glared before folding my arms. "Plus, that doesn't count. We just had a nap. A sleepover has to last until morning."

He arched a brow. "It was a four hour nap."

I shrugged. "I've had them."

"That's how long I usually sleep."

"Actually?" I paused, not knowing what to say. "Why not? Maybe you should listen to soothing music. Or crime podcasts. I've heard those do good."

"You've heard they're good?" He almost smirked.

Recognizing his accusation, I raised my hand in mock surrender. "Don't look at me. That stuff gives me nightmares. Nellie likes them though." This time, it was my turn to raise a brow. "And you didn't answer my question. Why can't you sleep long?"

Instead of answering, he lowered his chin so he focused his gaze between our bodies. Before I realized what was happening, his hand shot to mine and I gasped when I saw him gripping my little notebook.

"Myles! Give it back!" I hissed, throwing myself onto him but failing miserably. All he did was wrap a hand around my waist to keep me pinned on the wall. Baring my teeth, I hissed, "Myles!"

He smirked wickedly before flipping it open. The moment his eyes flickered over the first page, all the humour evaporated from his face. His hand pressed harder around my waist before he concentrated on me with a darkened expression.

Myles took a small step closer, seemingly taking all the air out of my lungs while never pulling his eyes off mine. "Nothing will come from this, princess."

I would have grinned in victory, had in not been for the fact that my body was preoccupied on the feeling of his hand touching me. Maybe it's shameful to admit, but I arched against the wall. I felt so depraved that I felt my body humming with desire. I didn't care that I could basically destroy this friendship before it could fully start. Maybe tomorrow, but not right now.

"Works with me." My smile felt sultry. And I was never sultry. "My roommates aren't home. They're at a hockey game."

"You didn't want to go with them?"

I smirked. "Wanna get dicked down, remember?"

He made a noise that seemed to combine a snarl and a harsh laugh. "Fuck. You're fucking insane, princess."

"I think that's evident." I pushed myself off the wall, and Myles dropped his hand off me. For now. I started walking toward the bright streets when I glanced over my shoulder and grinned. "Let's go. The faster we get there, the more stuff we can do. And the more things I can cross out from my list."

He narrowed his eyes and strode toward me. Once we were walking side by side, he glared in my direction. "I swear to fucking god, if you start saying what you're going to cross out mid-action, I'm leaving."

I laughed loudly. "I promise I won't!"

He made a grunting noise, like he didn't believe me.

Still, I noticed he was matching my fast pace back to my home. The closer we got, the more my heart hammered in my chest. For the next ten minutes, all I could think about was him touching me and I thanked the God's that it was dark out, so he wouldn't see my burning red cheeks. By the time I was unlocking my front door, I was basically sober.

My hands slightly shook as I pushed the door open. Once I kicked off my shoes, I tossed my jacket and Myles' hat on the bar stool and strode to the kitchen without looking back. I needed to do something, otherwise I'd go crazy.

"Do you want a drink?" I asked over my shoulder, not waiting for his response before pulling the water filter out of the fridge.

The moment I moved to open the top cabinet for two glasses, I froze when I felt Myles' body pressing against me, digging my stomach into the counter.

I lowered my hand to the counter and softly exhaled when I felt his head dipping next to mine. Even though I couldn't see his face, I swear I felt his lips pulling into a smirk.

When he didn't do anything right away, I joked, "Are you a man of words or actions, batman?"

"I'm just thinking what I should do first," he murmured roughly before his large hands clasped themselves around my waist. I shivered when a finger moved along my spine before his hand curled around my ponytail. He gave it a light tug and I instantly sucked a breath as my skin vibrated.

I closed my eyes. "You can do anything."

He gave a short, rough laugh. "Anything? Anal is on that list of yours, princess."

The moment I stiffened, he breathed out a short chuckle. His hand cupped the back of my neck before he moved toward my breast and squeezed. When his body molded against my back, I felt him poking my lower back and—oh my God he felt huge. My breathing was becoming erratic at this point.

His palm moved down my stomach in a painful pace before his fingers slithered inside my short dress. I arched against him and opened my mouth in a silent gasp when he started to tickle the inside of my thigh. I wasn't sure if he was going this slow to punish me, but I was seconds away from jumping him.

I told him exactly that.

His body stiffened against mine, and through my hazy mind, I came to the realization that maybe, he was giving me the chance to back out.

"I have a very low self-control, princess. Do you really wanna poke this bear?"

Yes. I want to poke this freaking bear.

"We're gonna be crossing more than one thing from your list, princess." I felt Myles' rough murmur travel through my body, right before his finger grazed my panties.

"Fuck me, Myles. Or I swear to all things holy—oh."

With one hand fisting my ponytail, he yanked my head back before he thrust two fingers deep enough inside me that I started quivering against the counter.

My head fell back, and all thoughts vanished when I felt his teeth biting my earlobe. A finger drifted over my clit and my hooded eyes closed with a shaky sigh before he wrapped an arm around my waist. A startled gasp left me when he suddenly hauled me off my feet. With one arm.

He never removed his fingers. The moment we were in my bedroom, he slammed the door behind us and spun me around. My vision blurred as my thigh hit a hard edge. Next thing I knew, I fell onto the mattress.

The air was knocked out from me, and I felt a chill running over me when I realized Myles' absence.

I started to open my eyes when Myles' hands began to cradle my head. "What are you—"

He shushed me, just as I felt a light material being wrapped around my eyes. I inhaled sharply when I opened my eyes, only to see darkness. Muscles weak, I tried to bring my hand toward the blindfold—not to pull it off, just out of curiosity—but I never got the chance. Myles snatched my wrists and lifted them above my head.

Coming to the realization of what he was doing, I felt myself getting wetter. And he wasn't even touching me. Number one and number six.

When Myles realized I wasn't pulling my arms back, his grip tensed a moment before he wrapped a soft material around my wrists until he deemed it tight enough. The headboard rattled, and I knew he was restraining me thoroughly.

After a moment, he moved back. Both curious and aroused, I tugged on the restraints, and sure enough, I was stuck.

The longer we sat in silence, the more my body arched in anticipation.

With my vision removed, all my senses heightened. I heard the floorboard softly creaking beneath Myles' feet as he moved around the foot of my bed. So close, but so far.

After a few painful seconds of hyper-awareness, I sucked in a breath when Myles twisted my panties around his fingers and yanked them down my legs. I opened my mouth to demand he hurry up, but he never gave me the chance before his hand slithered between my centre and jammed two fingers back inside me.

I cried out when he pinched my swollen clit and scissored his fingers inside me. He continued working my body like an instrument until I threw my head back and moaned as my body shook with a climax. I pulled on my restraints, and it only made me wetter.

Suddenly, two fingers were plunged into my mouth. It took me a second to realize Myles was feeding me my own release. Something I'd never done before, and yet, I still squeezed my eyes and sucked all the juices soaking his fingers.

When he shot his hand back, I could taste his struggle for control. He still hasn't spoken.

"Fuck, Althea. You fucking drenched my hand."

"Then do something about it." He snarled at my taunting tone, almost as if he was struggling to grasp the last of his control. Still blindfolded, I sagged against the bed and sighed, even though my body was still craving more. "If you want to stop, we can stop. The hockey game is probably ending soon anyways, so I'm sure the bars will be packed. I can have my choice of the litter. Guys who watch hockey are either really, really hot or really, really condescending. But, the combination might offer great sex. So untie me if you want to sto—"

My rant was cut short when his hands shot toward the top of my dress. He collected as much material as he could before he ripped the dress, straight down the middle.

Cold air swept over my body, and I felt my nipples pebble while I gasped for air. I heard something fall onto the ground, followed by a belt unbuckling. The sound was enough to make me pull on the restraints in anticipation. I heard a wrapper being torn followed by the mattress suddenly dipping. It was a matter of seconds before Myles' body loomed over me.

The mattress sank next to my head—most likely from him supporting himself up. He shoved his knee between my legs and sunk his fingers into my thigh before lifting my leg. When he jerked himself against my core, I shook with unconstrained desire.

"Myles..."

He laughed darkly, and the sound made my heart race faster. "Say what you want like a good slut. Beg for my cock."

My core clenched while I whimpered in surprise and embarrassment by how much I liked his crude demand. It was on my list, but no one ever spoke to me that way. Yet, I shamelessly seemed to love it, seeing how my body continued to try to push itself closer to Myles' touch.

Myles. Myles was saying these things to me. I think I've disconnected that my some-what of a friend was making me feel this way.

He only parted my thighs wider. Frigid air caressed my thighs before I felt his cock nestling between my legs. This time, my clit throbbed, needing relief.

His head dipped closer to my neck before he released my thigh and squeezed my breast. "Beg, Althea." He pinched my sensitive nipple, which helped me find my voice.

"Please fuck me, Myles." My sentence barely finished before he gripped my outer thigh and drove into me brutally. Angrily.

I braced my knee on his side and choked on a sob. Because Myles was big. Bigger than I've ever had. But despite the sting of pain, I felt my body zapping to life. Pain and pleasure intertwined itself, fulfilling me with a delicious feeling as he moved in and out.

"Fuck," I heard him clenching through his teeth before he angled my leg higher and deepened his thrusts. "Your cunt is squeezing me so good, princess."

I moaned breathlessly before his gripped my ponytail and jerked my head to the side, exposing my neck. His teeth scrapped my column of my throat. I pushed my body off the mattress in surprise when his mouth lowered to my breast and bit on my nipple.

Each thrust turned deeper. Harder. Until he's sliding almost all the way out and slamming in again. He reached a new depth that made my lips part in a silent scream. The sound of our bodies clashing only heightened my arousal before I wiggled my hips to get him in deeper.

He quickly noticed and coaxed, his hot breath brushing against my breast, "Such a greedy princess."

"Yes," I rasped and threw my head back, my mind fogged with pleasure.

I felt his smirk against my chest before he switched to the other nipple. He continued his powerful rhythm before he pulled his head away. Even though I was blindfolded, I knew his eyes were on me.

When he grinded against me, simultaneously rubbing against my pulsing clit, I opened my mouth in a muted gasp. I pulled on the restraints and came to the conclusion that these wouldn't be an every day occurrence. While I liked my body being controlled, I wanted to touch him. Feel the muscles that were rubbing against me.

Those thoughts vanished when he rested an ankle over his shoulder. "I want you to scream for me," he ordered with a sinister edge and pulled out almost all the way before slamming into me.

My entire body erupted in goosebumps when he bottomed out, reaching a part inside me I never knew existed. I made a noise, and Myles took that as a good sign, because he kept his hard pace and was rewarded with the sound getting louder each time, until I was crying out his name.

The moment his hand vanished between my thighs and pinched my clit, my climax slammed into me. My whole body convulsed as he pounded into me faster, chasing his own orgasm.

It wasn't long after I felt him pulse before he spilled into the condom while I softly rocked my hip against him unconsciously. His breathing came out ragged while my chest heaved. Slowly, my mind woke up with the realization of what we'd done before noticing he was still inside me.

I got wet all over again.

□□□·□ □·□□□

happy Friday loves :) happy HAPPY Friday to Myles and Althea too

I found a book series last night, but I fell asleep ASAP, so I couldn't fully enjoy it—now that I'm back from work.... I'm not going to sleep tonight, that's all I'm going to say

wishing you all the best, and I'll see you next week x

Chapter 9

C HAPTER IXBootie Call

□□□·□ □·□□□

Check.

Check.

Check.

With a grin ear to ear, I closed my small notebook and turned my attention to the window. Streaks of sun fell onto my bed, no thanks to my sheer curtains. But unlike other times, I didn't mind it. My body was completely relaxed—and sore. I was revelling in it.

I don't remember ever feeling so physically satisfied. Scratch that. I've never been satisfied by a man—at least, not without my help. I usually had to touch my clit, but Myles... this man had my hands tied and made me come four times last night. I didn't even know that could happen.

Glancing at the notebook in my lap, I bit my lip and wondered the next time I could cross more things out.

At the same time, I didn't want to push Myles' boundaries. He didn't seem too closed off last night when he finally finished. In fact, we ended up bantering the entire time he was putting his clothes on. It made me relieved, knowing that whatever... this was, it wouldn't affect our somewhat of a relationship.

A sudden knock on my door made me jolt out of my thoughts. Widening my eyes, I twisted my head toward the door. "Who is it?"

"Me," Nellie said before drawling, "You alone?"

That question confirmed my worst fear—well, not the worst one, but it was definitely up there. She heard me having sex. No one ever wanted their roommates, let alone their best friend, hear that. Especially when you didn't want to answer any questions.

Remembering that I currently held my sex list, I scrambled and shoved my notebook inside the first drawer of my nightstand before sitting against the headboard.

Clearing my throat, I embarrassingly rasped, "Yeah."

Despite me assuring her, she gently cracked the door open and double checked that my room was, in fact, empty.

She visibly sighed in relief before entering the room and closing the door behind her.

Her blonde hair was pulled in a high pony, and because she wore black yoga shorts, it made her tanned legs longer than usual. She also dressed in an oversized navy sweatshirt that hid most of her figure.

The moment, I finished my quick assessment, I met her nearly black, hooded eyes and cringed when I saw them in slits. The judgment was radiating off her.

"I can't believe you found a rebound without telling me."

My mouth opened until I mentally repeated what she said. That's what she was angry about.

Ignoring my shocked expression, she threw her arms up in frustration before continuing, "I mean, obviously I agreed you should get a rebound, but I thought you'd tell me everything." Her eyes widened in horror before they shot to mine. "Wait, was it with..."

"No. It was a guy from the bar," I lied easily. Way too easily. But I wanted to save myself from Nellie's rant that I was being unsafe. I knew what I was doing, and right now, it didn't want to feel criticized. Nellie would come from a good place—she always cared, but I wanted a moment of peace.

Considering the last time she saw Myles, he had a gun pointed at her, I didn't want to ruin the moment. Even though the memory still scarred me, his intentions weren't with malice.

Nellie stared at me silently. "Was he good?"

Her curiosity made me grin. "Very good." Hearing that, she softened her face before sitting on the edge of my bed. "How did you know..."

"Hun, you guys were still going at it when I got home."

I flinched and slapped myself in the face. "Did Val—"

"Her car wasn't in the driveway when I got home. And your dude left less than an hour later. I don't think she came home last night, to be honest."

There was a part of me that was worried. Why didn't Val come home? Was she okay? But I did my best to withhold the urge to text and ask. At least, for now.

"So," Nellie began slowly, and I knew I had to prepare myself for what she had to say next. "Are you still talking to that guy? Myles?"

Knowing where this was going, I tightly smiled. "Nels—"

"Seriously, Allie?" She gaped when she read my guilty expression. "You're still talking to him? After what he did?"

"He explained himself," I weakly defended. "He said he grew up in a bad area and wears a gun to protect himself. He feels bad." Well, he didn't say that, but I know he did.

She arched a brow. "But he's still going to hold it? Carry it around you? Did you even try to compromise?"

"Not explicitly—"

"Allie," she cried in frustration and disappointment. "What if, God forbid, you startle him and he pulls a gun on you? What if his reflexes are too fast, and he doesn't realize that he shot you until it's too late?"

Her words painted a visual in my mind. Her chin tilted in satisfaction when I flinched.

"I'll talk to him," I said after a moment, taking her words to heart. "Don't worry. I know how to take care of myself. He means well, Nels. I know he looks a little... cold, but I promise he's really sweet when he opens up. Okay, not really sweet, but he's different than how he looks. I told you he helped me get home that night." He defended me in front of Remi. He walked to the club with me when I couldn't get on his motorcycle. He's given me his hat. He watched Toy Story, even though he adamantly stated he'd never watch Disney. And despite him stupidly starting a fight, he did it because he felt defensive for me.

But I didn't say those things, because somehow, they felt more personal.

Nellie's shoulders sagged before letting out a defeated sigh. "I just don't want you to make any stupid mistakes that you might regret."

"Anything can be a mistake, Nels," I told her with a small smile. "If you don't do something just because you might regret it later, life would be really, really boring."

"But it'd also be safe," she retorted.

"Safe is boring." Throwing the blanket off me, I stood from my bed with wobbly legs. I was grateful that I slipped into shorts and a tee before falling asleep. "I think ending things with Remi made me realize how I've been playing everything safe. I wanna take risks, you know?"

She watched me silently, and I knew she didn't completely agree. Still, I stopped in front of her and held her shoulders while tipping my head back, so our eyes remained locked.

"If you don't get it, at least support me. This is our last semester, and I wanna end it with a bang. Literally."

That forced a grin out of her. "I hope the sex sexually liberates you, Allie. And I'd kill a bitch for you, so make sure you tell that to anyone who thinks it's smart enough to hurt you while you... take risks."

"Aw, Nels," I cooed and pulled her into a tight hug. "I love you."

She grumbled underneath her breath but wrapped her arms around me, nonetheless.

When we ended up separating, Nellie expressed that she'd meet me at class because she needed to do some errands beforehand. Since I had two hours until class started, I got dressed and ate some breakfast before heading out to buy some coffee. By the time I was waiting in line to order, class would begin in an hour.

As I placed my order, I glanced out the window and lingered my eyes on the tattoo shop that employed Myles'. Before I could stop myself, I ordered him a coffee as well.

There was a high chance he wasn't inside, since he mentioned that he started work at one. But I hoped I might catch him with an earlier client, so I could drop the coffee off.

Once I held two rippled cups of coffee, I strode outside, just as a cool chill attacked my face.

I made sure there weren't any cars driving nearby before crossing the street in a slight jog. I tried to focus on the glass door, only to grin when I saw a tattooed woman sitting behind the podium. Holding the cups with one hand, I reached out and opened the door, which rang from my entrance.

The woman glanced up from whatever she was going on the computer with a bored expression. Her eyes drifted to any exposed skin I had—which wasn't much, considering my jacket was zipped up to my neck.

"You lost? Or do you wanna tat your virgin skin?"

"Not lost, just dropping off something," I grinned but quickly furrowed my brows. "Is it that obvious that I have no tattoos?"

The woman, who looked like she was in her late-twenties, smirked. "Something about you, girl. I can just tell." She leaned back and cocked her head. "What you dropping off? And for who?"

For a moment, I inspected the woman's black hair. It was short and choppy, but still appeared styled. She also seemed incredibly short, but her height didn't stop her from being intimidating. Because she dressed in a tank top and jeans, I noticed tattoos covering her entire right arm, and some on her left. One that I kept lingering on, however, was the opened cage on her bicep. Birds were escaping and flying on her collarbone and neck.

"Girl?" Her tone was questioning, which reminded me that I never answered her question.

Smiling apologetically, I adjusted the cups in my hands. "Myles. Do you know if he's here?"

Her smirk was whipped off her face. "You're here for Myles?" This time, her gaze became scrutinizing. "Really? He knock you up or something?"

I choked on spit. "What? N-no."

The woman didn't seem to believe me. Yet, something settled over her expression. Almost a mixture of interest and amusement. "Well, he's in the back. Probably carving."

She strode away from the desk when I repeated, "Carving?"

Her eyes rolled back, but not in a, I'm judging you, kind of way. I could tell when I saw her dark painted lips twitch.

"Outlining the tat. Customer only got in twenty minutes ago."

So he was here. I sighed in relief and followed her to the back of the studio. Because the last time I was here, Myles hauled me to the back office, I finally had the opportunity to look around and check out my surroundings. There seemed to be a Dark Scandinavian theme in the open concept room.

The walls were painted a dark grey, but there were hardly empty spaces. Most of the room had frames in different shapes and sizes filling up the walls. The photos seemed to consist of tattoo sketches, but there were some that had pictures of rock bands I was unfamiliar with. In the front of the studio, there was a floor-to-ceiling mirror that stretched out four feet, which impressed me.

There was a single pathway to the end of the parlour—which I knew led to the back office. However, there were five tattoo chairs—which I could see, because the grey curtains were open. There were three on my right, but as I trailed my gaze to the left, I noticed a closed curtain at the back-left corner of the studio. Even though the curtain must have been thick, I could see bright light seeping from its confides.

The woman was leading me straight there.

"Yo, Scar."

Scar? Was she taking me to see Myles?

The moment she started to open the curtain, I heard a hard voice bite gruffly, "Get the fuck out, Chloe."

Even though her back was to me, I could tell by her voice that she was glaring. "Low, asshat." Pushing her shoulders back, she started to open the curtain wider. "You gotta visitor."

Now able to see Myles, I frowned when I saw him hunched over a guys beefy arm, holding a black marker. He never lifted his head up, and I debated on leaving. He was obviously busy.

"Tell Spike to leave me the fuck alone. I don't have time for his shit."

"It ain't Spike. It's a girl." She said the last word with so much amusement, as if she couldn't believe that someone of the opposite sex was visiting him.

Myles' hand stopped its even strokes on the man's skin. There was a collective moment of silence before Myles tipped his head back and met my gaze.

There was a flicker of surprise before it disappeared. I couldn't help but clench my legs together when memories of last night returned. Especially when some strands of his hair escaped the confides of his bun and hovered at the sides of his face.

Feeling unnerved by his intense stare, I lifted the hand that was holding his coffee. "I got you something."

That was enough to pull him out from his thoughts.

Sitting upright, he twisted his head toward Low and stated blankly, "You can go now."

I narrowed my eyes at his rude tone, but Low clearly must have been used to his behaviour because she just shrugged before stepping away from the curtain. The man on the chair said nothing until Myles shot up from his seat.

"I'll be back, Jeff."

He didn't wait for his clients reply before rounding the chair and heading straight for my direction. I yelped in surprise when he dropped a hand to my lower back and guided me to the back office.

The moment the door closed behind us, I moved away from his hand and faced him with a grin. He didn't turn the light on—not that he needed to. The open window brought enough light for me to read his guarded expression.

"For you."

When he didn't take the coffee out from my grip right away, I brought it closer to his chest.

He concentrated on my face before asking deeply, "What's this for?"

"A thank you!" I grinned, jerking it closer to him. "Take it."

For the first time today, his lip rose in a slight smirk. "You bought me coffee because I fucked you, princess?"

"Buying coffee for other people is my love language, if you haven't noticed." He stiffened at the word love, making me widen my eyes in fear. "No! I don't love you! I mean, you're a cool guy and whatever, but when I say love language, I mean it applies to my friends. I buy coffee for my friends. I don't know what my love language would be if I was in a relationship. Looking back with Remi, there wasn't much I could say I loved. That kinda sounds mean, doesn't it?"

Now full on cringing, I lowered the cup to his hand and forced him to grab it. "Take it. I'm going to slap myself."

"Don't slap yourself." Still, I heaved in relief when he finally wrapped his fingers around the cup. "Thank you."

His appreciation stopped me from abusing my face.

I looked his way again and smiled. "No problem."

Myles didn't take his eyes off me while he brought the cup to his mouth. The moment he took a sip, he jerked his head in surprise and lowered his head to the cup. He read the label with furrowed brows.

"What..." He shook his head in disbelief before meeting my gaze. "How do you know my order?"

"I, uh... remembered it? You know, after I found about about Remi, you went into a cafe and I heard you order a medium latte. You're don't seem like the type to impulsively order new drinks every time you go to a cafe, so I figured that's your regular order."

He said nothing, but my heart thumped a little fast when I saw his expression sobering as his eyes slowly moved around me.

We stood in silence until he took a long sip, his eyes never peeling off mine.

"Are you sore?"

Just like that, my cheeks burned with colour.

Despite the initial embarrassment I felt from his question, there was a tingle of desire between my legs. I thought about what would happen if I said no, just to have sex again. To cross more things off my list.

The idea must have made my body spiral in fear because when I shifted in my spot, I felt a sharp pain coming from my core. My grimace brought out a dark smirk from Myles. He was clearly pleased with himself.

I opened my mouth to say... I didn't know what I was going to say. Most likely let my mouth run wild and change the topic. But I never got the chance to worsen my embarrassment because in the next second, my phone rang from my jacket pocket.

Mumbling a quick apology, I fished out my phone and internally groaned when I read mom's contact ID. I was tempted to ignore her, but she rarely ever called, so I assumed it was something important.

Smiling apologetically, I rushed out, "Give me a minute," before answering the call. "Hey, mom."

Myles didn't seem impatient or annoyed. In fact, he twitched his head and kept his eyes on me, almost with curiosity. He took a long gulp of his coffee when I heard mom chirp, "Hi, sweetie. How are you doing?"

"Good, how's your trip?"

I fidgeted on my spot from the intensity of Myles' attention. He must have noticed by now, but he didn't shy away from watching me. Hell, he was probably hiding a satisfied smile behind the cup.

"Good," she said almost breathlessly before swiftly adding, "I can't talk too long. Your father and I are just about to head for dinner, but I wanted to call you first to tell you we're coming back at the end of March."

I tried to smile, but all I felt was sick. "Oh yeah?"

"We're hoping you come by for dinner. To catch up. We actually have some exciting news to share with you!" She sounded to happy, but the idea of sitting with my parents, alone, made me want to crawl into a hole.

Did they really want to eat dinner with me? Or did they feel like they had to, out of obligation?

These depressive thoughts were shoved deep into my unconscious because I refused to think about how my parents might feel about me. But despite my best efforts, I knew my face expressed everything I was thinking. Myles' increasingly worrying expression confirmed that.

Well, as worried as he could be. The man struggled to display typical emotions.

"Sure, mom." My efforts to lace excitement in my tone failed. This time, Myles narrowed his eyes.

Mom, however, didn't notice anything. "Great, sweetie. I'll send you message with more updates soon! It'll be around the last week of March, so just keep your schedule open." There was a muffled noise in the background, followed by mom's light giggle. "I'll let you go now. Have a great day, sweetie."

The moment the call ended, I let out a breath.

"The fuck was that about, princess?" Myles asked, almost angrily. I flung my head back in surprise, so he added, "You look like they just told you someone died."

"Yeah, my sanity," I grumbled automatically before cringing. I hastily lifted my head and forced a smile when my eyes met Myles' glare. He didn't soften his expression; clearly reading through my facade.

"It's not a big deal. They were just inviting me for dinner in a few weeks. They're coming back from their trip," I explained to fill the tension. But when I started, I couldn't stop. "I think I told you about that, right? That they've been travelling since my mom's birthday. Which is in November, so you can imagine how long they've been gone. I mean, it was kinda depressing that they didn't come back for Christmas, but I celebrated with Nellie. Her family moved back to Romania, so we did something the two of us. Wait, that also kinda sounds depressing, but I promise it was kinda fun. We watched Hallmark Christmas movies. You think Disney movies suck, wait till you watch those. But I eat them up. Nellie, on the other hand, was dying from disgust. She doesn't like bad acting and claims she's allergic to it, but I just think she's being dramat... Myles. Shut me up."

The only reason I managed to stumble away from my rant was because he looked seconds away from exploding with laughter.

"I hate you."

He kept the smug look on his face, so I decided to pull out my—metaphorical—list of questions, simply to annoy him.

"So, who's Spike?"

Just like that, all of his amusement dried up and was tossed out the window.

His face was blank before he roughly asked, "How do you know that name?"

Gradually lifting the coffee to my mouth, I took a long sip while keeping my eyes locked on his. He seemed slightly irritated, which only made me smirk.

"You did think I was Spike when I came up to you." His face tightened, but he didn't satisfy me with a response. "Well? Who is he? Brother? Father?

Uncle? Grandpa? Oh, granduncle? Wait... is a granduncle your grandpa's brother? I don't know why I just thought of that." I shook my head, forcing myself to get back on track. "Anyway. Who is he? And is he actually named Spike, or is that a nickname?"

"Jesus fucking Christ." I grinned at his frustration. He glared at my mouth before focusing on me again. "He's my mentor."

"Mentor? A tattoo mentor? He taught you how to tattoo?"

"Yes."

I pursed my lips in thought, ignoring his short answers. "And his name? Actually, no. Your name. Low called you Scar. Why did she call you that?"

His walls built up so fast that I didn't realize it was happening until it was too late. Next thing I knew, he pushed his shoulders back and stalked to the exit.

"I think that's enough questions, princess. You already got a decent chunk of money in the jar."

I stomped my foot in anger. "We're not actually doing that!" I pointed a stern finger at him. "Swear jar!"

He said nothing as he threw the door open, and I glared at his back the whole time as he left the room.

Both annoyed and confused, I left the tattoo studio without peering to-ward Myles—who was already hidden behind the curtain. However, as I stepped outside and came face to face with a cold blast of wind, I mentally scrolled through my list of questions and answers I'd gotten from Myles.

Only to realize, that even when he does answer my questions, another five come in its place.

Myles-what's-his-last-name is an enigma that I'm desperately going to solve.

□□□·□ □·□□□

Today was my last day of work :') it's a sad day

but at the same time... I FINALLY HAVE TIME TO WRITE... until the new year, then back to school for me

wishing you the best Friday x

9 781787 991941